Enemies
OFF CAMERA

FLAMING
HEARTS
PRESS

ISBN: 978-1-963546-26-2

ONE

THE FINAL ONE-ON-ONE
DINNER DATE

Nothing fills me with happiness more than knowing this is almost over. I can almost taste the end. The cameras are far enough away to make it seem like this little scene is real, but close enough to remind me it's all a show. A very stupid reality show, in my opinion.

The show's called *The Final Play*. It matches star athletes with the partner of their dreams. That's all I knew when I signed on. My agent pitched it to me at the last minute after one of the original contestants backed out. And now here I am, a contestant vying for the heart of the heartless. Not by choice. Long story—one that starts with bad press and ends with a contract I should've read twice.

"Look alive," Betty, my producer, says through my earpiece.

Her request falls on deaf ears. I'm done. Burned out. Over it. I've been here six weeks. And every time Jax Wilde pins a golden rose on me because he's *supposedly* interested, I know he's just being facetious. A jerk, really.

But Betty's right—it's my job to think of something to say. After long, soul-draining conversations with the other nineteen contestants—now down to three, two after tonight—I've confirmed I'm the only real actress in the bunch. So it's my job to act like I like him.

I paste on my fake smile and googly eyes—the ones I'm tired of seeing in the mirror.

Jax Wilde, star wide receiver for the San Diego Bull Sharks, is already glaring at me.

"So, when are you going to say it?" he asks. The corner of his mouth hikes up into an arrogant smirk.

"Say what?" I snap. He's given me permission to drop the act.

"Thank me for choosing you to sit down for this spread." He gestures grandly at the table, arms outstretched, as if he's presenting a royal feast.

I hadn't even noticed the display: smoked lobster tails, prawns boiled, baked, and fried in crispy batter, crab legs piled high with tangy sauces and mouthwatering sides. You'd think I'd care; I've been dreaming of the day I could take myself out somewhere truly fancy—five stars, Michelin chef, the whole deal. But right now, it all barely registers.

I fold my arms. "Did you buy it?"

He leans back in his chair, eyes narrowing to slits. Gorgeous brown eyes, according to the other girls. Me? I barely notice them. Then suddenly, as if possessed by a tornado, he lunges forward.

"Okay, you miserable—" He cuts himself off, but I know what he wants to say.

I lean in too. Our faces nearly meet over the pile of crab legs.

"You mean *bitch*," I say for him. "Because I am a bitch, and so are you."

"Alright, knock it off!" Betty yells in my ear.

And by the look on his face, I can tell Kim, his producer, just chewed him out too.

This always happens when we're in a scene together.

"You know your lines. Now say them," Betty says.

I stop glaring and erase every insult from my mind. Straighten my back. Deep breath.

"You look beautiful tonight," he says before I can speak.

Bullshit. He doesn't think I look beautiful. I'm not even his type; he's made that painfully clear more than once. And, well, ditto.

This is a romance.

I am the heroine.

I am in love.

I am in awe.

This man is not an asshole.

"Thank you," slips off my tongue like honey. I barely recognize my own voice. "And look at this delicious food, I…" My mouth freezes mid-sentence as laughter threatens to burst free.

"I…" I try again. My lips quiver. I close my eyes. *Don't laugh, Zara.*

"Can't think of anyone else I'd rather share it with," I blurt, too fast—and then it happens. I burst out laughing.

Jax shakes his head like I've failed not only him, but the crew, the show, and maybe even myself.

"Really?" Betty groans in my ear.

I laugh harder. "But I *can* think of someone better to share this with. Something, actually. Like that fly buzzing around it."

"You know what?" Jax shoots to his feet. "I'm out. Bring this shit to my room—I'm eating it alone." He jabs a finger at me. "And don't give her any."

And that makes me laugh even harder.

What a jerk.

TWO

5 HOURS LATER

When I returned from our date, Heather and Ashley wanted to hear all about it. The cameras were rolling. I didn't want to look those poor, sweet airheads in the eyes and lie —but I did.

I told them we had a lovely, tasty dinner of seafood. Too bad I don't eat seafood, which is why I'm currently inhaling the catered Thai food in the kitchen. Bright-eyed, small-faced Ashley wanted to know if Jax and I kissed. The first words that came to mind were *hell no*, but instead I leaned in and whispered in her ear, "Don't worry, darling—he's all yours."

She lit up like a harvest moon. I was glad to give her that.

Ashley, with her tiny high-pitched voice and Disney-character looks, has been Jax's favorite from the start. Of course she's his type. She's every guy's type. *Bubbly.* Men love that word.

"She's bubbly," they say, like it's a personality trait and not just the sound of her laugh echoing in their skulls.

Then I took a plate piled high with carbs and carried it to my room—which, thankfully, I now share with nobody but myself—and ate. With a full belly made from guilt-free gorging (I'll worry about my diet when I'm back on the set of a real TV show or movie), I went straight to bed.

BAM, BAM, BAM...

Someone's knocking on my door like they're the cops. The vibration ripples through me, and I sit up, rubbing my eyes.

"Zara?" a familiar voice calls.

"What is she doing here?" I whisper, blinking hard. Maybe I'm dreaming.

"I'm coming in," she says—and then in walks Anna Park, my agent.

One look at Anna and I feel a wave of resentment. She reeks of the outside world—the place I want to be right now.

"What are you doing here?" I ask, then glance at the clock on my nightstand. It's 11:33 p.m.

Anna is wearing jeans and a Bruins sweatshirt. I've never seen her dressed so casually—and she's been my agent for three years. She looks exhausted. Deep purple digs in under both eyes, and she's not even trying to hide them. Her neat bob is pulled back in a ponytail, exposing her pale, bloodless face.

I clutch at my rapidly beating heart, convinced I've screwed up my comeback after that dinner disaster.

"What's going on?" I ask, short of breath. *Six weeks down the drain because of one bad dinner. Stupid me.*

She sighs, long and forceful. "I've got some good news," she says, and I perk up. "And a qualifier of that good news."

I wrinkle my nose. "A qualifier?"

"Heather's been sent home. It was filmed. That was the deal with the dinner. Jax had to choose between you and her."

"Dinner was a disaster. He should've sent me home, not Heather." I scrunch up my face and shake my head. "He knows he's getting under my skin."

Anna grunts like I've said the wrong thing, then folds her arms.

"Didn't you hear me say I have good news? Heather is gone, and you're a finalist for a reason, Zara. You haven't figured it out yet."

"Figured out what?"

This time, her arms drop like the weight of her entire day just sank into the floor.

"You have five million new followers on social media since this gig," she says. "And you've been cast as the sister in a new Rowan TV series called *Next In Line*. It's kind of like *Succession*, but grittier. It's a major role."

My jaw drops. I want to scream with joy—but the way she delivers the news, so dryly, makes me pause.

I square my shoulders. "Okay... what else?"

There's a look in Anna's eyes I don't trust. I've seen it before. She's thinking. Or rather—trying to outthink me.

"Zara..." she says, walking over and sitting beside me on the rock-hard bed. "I barely inked this deal for you. We're back, but you did not make this easy. And I don't want you ruining it. So go to wardrobe, get your makeup on, and play your part. It's time for the final pin."

Silence falls. I'm still confused.

"Is that the qualifier?" I ask. "I mean... after tonight, this is over, right?"

Her lips curl into a big smile.

"Indeed it is. So..." — she pauses — "I want you to have all the right reactions. Got it? Your future depends on it."

THREE

1 HOUR LATER

The scene is bustling. Crew members, as tired as usual, move around setting up lights, cameras, and set pieces. I can't take my eyes off the final pins. Something about Anna's visit still doesn't sit right with me.

I turn to her—she's still here, on set, locked in deep conversation with Betty. Neither of them looks my way, even when I try to catch their eyes.

"I'm going to miss you so much," Ashley says sweetly.

I jump, startled. I didn't hear her walk up beside me. When I finally pull my attention away from Pinky and the Brain across the room—plotting something about me—and look at Ashley, I nearly gasp.

She's devastatingly beautiful tonight. No wonder Jax's been crushing on her since day one. I mean, she *looks* like a Disney princess.

We hug. Her body is so delicate in my arms, like she might break.

"Me too," I say. "If you ever need to send an SOS to escape the catastrophe about to go down, I'll be your knightess in shining armor."

"Oh, Zara," she chuckles softly. "He's not *that* bad. You just don't like him for some reason. It's odd."

I open my mouth to defend myself point by point, but… what's the point, at this juncture?

This ridiculous show is almost over.

We're in our pretty gowns, faces full of makeup, itchy extensions reattached to our scalps. I just can't see the logic in Jax choosing me, so I won't ruin what should be a fabulous night—for Ashley—when he picks her, and I can finally go home, soak in my tub, and sleep in my own bed.

That's all Anna wants from me—just the right reaction to the final pinning. I get it. I'll play along. I'll clap and cry and hug Ashley. I'll shake Jax's hand and say, *Well done.*

No…

I have to *look* like I've lost. Like I'm *disappointed* by the outcome.

I'll hug him. Loosely. I don't want his body on mine for too long. And when I'm asked how I feel, I'll say, *"Hurt, of course, but I always knew she was the one."*

That's what a girl's girl would say. And I've worked hard to establish myself as one of those.

"You okay?" Ashley asks.

She looks genuinely concerned. While my thoughts were racing, I'd been standing here looking completely stupefied.

I close my mouth and force a smile that gradually becomes real as fantasies of freedom start to wash over me. "I'm fine. Congratulations."

"You know… he could choose you," Ashley says, though there's no real conviction in her eyes.

The thought makes my stomach nosedive. I can't shake how worried I am about that possibility.

My gaze shifts back to Anna and Betty—but they're no longer where they were. Maybe that's a good sign. Maybe my central nervous system is just getting the best of me.

Still, I've been turning over the question in my mind: *How could Jax choosing me possibly benefit the both of us?*

Me? Sure. I'm a PR disaster, and any attention— even fake love on a fake show—is great for my career.

But Jax? He's no PR mess, at least not that I know of. Why else would he be cast as the show's Knight in Shining Armor if he were?

"We'll start recording in fifteen," Hansel, the show's director, announces over the loudspeaker.

Ashley and I lock eyes, wide and nervous. She takes my hands and squeezes them.

"No matter what, let's stay friends, okay? I know you don't like him, but I like *you*. I'll be your referee—and I'll be fair."

I give her a tight smile as she laughs at her own big-hearted promise. The thing is, what I *want* to say is: *I don't ever want to see his face again. Ever.*

But I'm spared from having to let her down gently as we're called to our spots under the soft, flattering lights.

As makeup and wardrobe put the finishing touches on our appearance, Jax enters the stage.

Beside me, Ashley gasps—sharp enough to reveal exactly what's on her mind. She thinks he looks handsome.

I've seen more handsome men. I've *dated* more handsome men. Good-looking guys are a dime a dozen. It's what's inside that matters.

Still… objectively speaking, Jax *is* handsome in a black suit that fits him in all the right places. Most women would like—no, *love*—his hypnotic bedroom eyes and chiseled jawline.

So yeah. He's good-looking. *So what.*

What really gets me is his expression.

Usually, he'll toss Ashley a wink or a smirk—some little breadcrumb to let her know she's his gal.

I gnaw nervously on my bottom lip.

"Don't do that, Kara," Janet, the makeup artist, scolds.

I grunt and roll my eyes as she wipes red lipstick off my teeth and reapplies it.

Something's off. Jax isn't acting like his usual cocky, spotlight-loving self. The one who relishes rejecting a hopeful contestant he clearly thinks is beneath him.

Oh…

I exhale slowly, the tension easing in my shoulders.

He's not being smug because he's not about to break a heart tonight—*not mine*, anyway. He knows I'm not in love. He knows I won't be heartbroken.

Good. That makes two of us.

I stretch my neck from side to side. *Soon. Very soon.* I'm only minutes away from freedom. I've already made a vow: I will *never* do another reality show again. Ever.

"Everybody take your places!" the director calls.

Chaos buzzes around us.

I glance at Ashley—she looks nervous for the first time tonight.

Smiling, I wink at her and nod toward Jax, hoping to put her at ease. *He's yours, lady. He's all yours.*

Soon, it's quiet on set. *Action* has been called.

"Welcome to the final pinning ceremony," Dave Lyons says, stepping into frame.

Dave—our handsome host—is so much shorter than Jax that they're never filmed standing next to each other without Dave standing on a platform.

He launches into his usual monologue about *our*

13

journey to love. How "bumpy" the road has been for *both* ladies, which makes me grimace. *Bumpy for Ashley? No. For me? Yes. What is he even talking about?*

"But Ashley and Zara," Dave continues, "have both captured our Knight in Shining Armor's heart. And now, Jax, the time has come to pin the lady of your dreams."

Dave nods dramatically—he really is a good host for this kind of gig—and turns to face us.

My heart patters like heavy rain.

Something's not right. Jax isn't smiling at Ashley. He's looking straight at *me*. His gaze is long and deep, like he's trying to telepathically tell me something.

What the hell is going on?

My head spins as he picks up the final golden pin.

"Zara." He clears his throat. Then smiles.

It's a fake smile—I know it too well. The same one he's worn through every forced interaction we've ever had. The smile we practiced.

"Would you please…"

I shake my head instinctively.

No. No no no no no.

"Stop shaking your head!" Betty shouts in my earpiece.

Then Anna's voice follows, even louder. "Smile! Don't you drop the ball, Zara. Your *career* depends on it!"

"Huh?" I whisper, barely able to get the word out.

Because Jax has asked to pin *me*.

And the world is spinning.
Faster.
So fast—
I lose my footing.
And the next thing I know, I'm falling.
Everything goes dark.

FOUR

TWO WEEKS LATER

Needless to say, I've been trapped in a nightmare ever since Jaxon Wilde of the San Diego Bull Sharks chose me to be his partner.

I've been hiding out at home. All cast members are still under NDA, banned from exposing anything about the production. Which means I can't post, I can't vent, and I definitely can't explain myself—not even to Ashley.

Poor Ashley. I heard that right after I passed out, she ran off set and refused to return. Neither of our producers threw contracts in our faces or demanded we finish the scene strong. It was a wrap. When I came to, she was already gone.

We never exchanged numbers. I tried requesting her on several social platforms, but she followed each one with a block.

Needless to say, she's mad.

Maybe she thinks I knew Jax would pick me. And... if I'm being honest—deep down—I did.

It's the only thing that explains Anna showing up at the house in clothes that looked like she was dashing out for NyQuil at 11 p.m. Of course she didn't tell me the plan. If she had, I would've caused such a ruckus...

Or maybe not.

Who am I kidding? My career *is* very important to me.

Tonight, the final episode of the season airs.

Tomorrow, Jax and I—who haven't seen each other since before I hit the floor—will meet in Anna's office in Century City to discuss... whatever.

I've been practicing avoidance like it's an Olympic sport. Cocooned in my little house in Encino. A quaint cottage with tall trees shading its farmhouse windows and French doors. It was my first real purchase from my acting career. My escape from the world beyond my property's borders.

But I can't hide out forever. It's time to face the music.

I settle into a warm bubble bath, aim the remote at the TV mounted on the bathroom wall, and prepare to finally binge the series. I'm especially eager to see how production managed to spin *me* as the winner—considering our first interaction, which is also when I decided I hated him, was an unmitigated disaster.

Here goes nothing.

FIVE

The first few seconds of the show begin, and I'm already triggered. My breathing slows. All I want to do is turn the TV off.

But I can't. I have to watch.

What still baffles me is how I was declared the winner without loyal fans storming the network with pitchforks and foaming outrage.

First up: Heather, playing the theme from *Titanic* on her flute.

Thank God I wasn't around for that. I would've exploded with laughter—like I am now.

"What the hell is going on?" I manage to say between tears, wiping my eyes.

Then comes Lilith from San Diego, reciting a poem.

"Roses are red,
Violets are blue,

If you pick me,
I'll pick you."
Dear God.

Embarrassing. And desperate.

Which Lilith absolutely was—right up until the second pinning ceremony, when her eagerness finally became too much for even Jaxon. Letting her go was the kindest thing he did all season.

Still, I can't deny it: every girl's introduction was solid TV. Watching it now, it almost feels like any one of them had a real shot with the guy from hell. And Jaxon plays the role of the noble bachelor—our so-called knight in shining armor—so well. Too well.

Of course, anyone using their prefrontal cortex knows that kind of man is a myth.

I can't take it anymore. I skip ahead.

Jaxon and my first introduction is the one scene I've been dreading. The only meet-and-greet that went tragically wrong.

I fast-forward until I see myself emerge from the backseat of the limo.

A wave of prickles rushes through my skin—and not just because I've been in the tub too long.

There I am.

My red gown hugs my body like it was sewn on. Cap sleeves, high slit. My hair is pulled back from my face, the rest cascading in big, sand-colored curls behind me. Tiffany, my designated hair stylist, hated the way it turned out—mostly because I arrived four hours late to call time.

I wasn't even sure I was going to go through with the show. The night before, I watched two episodes from the previous season before realizing I couldn't stomach any more. The desperation for one man? Pathetic, actually.

But what was I going to do? Not show up? Give up on my comeback? Let the world keep thinking I'm the "crazy actress" who stole for no reason at all?

I squeeze my eyes shut tight. Just thinking about what happens next makes me sink deeper into the water, wishing I could disappear beneath the surface.

Regardless... I look pretty. Stunning, even. Jaxon raises his eyebrows and smiles—all teeth—like he's impressed.

But that's not what happened.

I was there. I know.

He stiffened as I approached. Then he looked away, turned to the pit of producers, and said:

"Really? You're giving me the shoplifting actress?"

That's what he said.

I stopped in my tracks, gasping.

After a beat, I snapped. "What did you call me?"

"You shoplifted. That's a crime, isn't it?"

"You arrogant, classless prick. This is a *TV show*. I'm pretty sure you're not the—" I threw up air quotes, "—*Prince Charming* they're trying to pass you off as. You asshole!"

I screamed that last part at the top of my lungs, fists clenched, head thrown back.

"Cut!" Hansel, the director, yelled.

We were both pulled aside—me to Betty, him to his producer.

Betty reminded me of the role I agreed to play. *Stick to the plan,* she said. *Do this right, and your career will smell like roses.*

And of course, I agreed.

I don't know what Jake, Jaxon's producer, said to him, but he came back with a reluctant apology.

"That was rude of me. I'm sorry," he said with zero conviction.

We were told to smile. So we did. Sort of.

I tried. But the more I forced it, the more my lips trembled.

Jaxon just sighed, over and over, like *I* had let *him* down.

I was humiliated. Not just because he embarrassed me, but because I'm an actress. A damn good one. I was almost nominated for an Emmy—twice, I was told.

But what he said... it cut deep. It triggered something in me. My nervous system went haywire. I couldn't recover. We couldn't get the shot.

Eventually, Hansel gave up and said he'd fix it in post.

And oh boy… did he ever.

I sit up straighter in the tub, pushing toward the front to get a better look.

That woman on the screen? It's definitely me.

"You look handsome tonight," I say.

But I never said that.

"Whoa… You're the first princess who's taken my breath away," Jaxon croons.

My jaw drops.

He's never said that to me. Not once.

"I can't wait to know you better," I say, eyes flirting.

Then I offer him my hand.

He takes it. Kisses it.

I gasp. "Holy shit," I whisper, eyes glued to the screen.

I blink hard.

Maybe I'm imagining this.

"What the hell?" I glance toward my bedroom, where my phone sits on the dresser.

I need to call my agent, Anne Kim.

I start to rise—then stop myself.

No.

I have to see the rest first.

I carefully step out of the tub, pause the video, dry off, and get dressed.

Because something tells me I'm about to find out *exactly* why I—or this fake version of me—won the final pin.

SIX

My eyes are wired, head unsettled. I'm exhausted, but there's no way I can sleep. It's like I'm tweaking or something.

What the hell am I watching?

And they were slick with the edits between Jaxon and me.

Like the group brunch date at that comedy club—I knew they wouldn't show what really happened there.

When Jaxon walked in to greet us, all the women applauded. Except me. Of course.

The producers didn't even prompt it. They were just that smitten. Though I think it had less to do with Jaxon himself and more to do with triumphing over the competition.

He noticed I didn't clap. Narrowed his eyes at me.

I returned the glare. The room went dead silent as we locked into an unspoken standoff, neither of us willing to be the first to look away.

"Stop it," Betty hissed in my ear.

"Tell him first," I whispered through clenched teeth like a trained ventriloquist.

Jake must've reined him in, because he finally turned to the rest of his harem and said, with all the confidence of a frat king:

"Ladies, the spread looks good, huh? But don't forget your girlish figures."

They giggled.

I gasped. Loudly. The only one offended.

"Cut," Hansel called.

And once again, claimed he'd "fix it in post."

Which is why I just watched myself giggling with the rest of them.

I've said "WTF" so many times over the past six hours, the letters are permanently etched into my brain.

Four weeks in, Jaxon took me on our first one-on-one date. We went bike riding.

The first thing he said to me was:

"Okay, hot fingers, why'd you do it?"

"Screw you," I snapped.

"Cut!" Hansel shouted.

"What?" I threw my hands up. "I didn't even say the F-word!"

We reset. The crew was exhausted by then—tired

of our constant sniping. Both of us were told to try again, nicer this time.

I remember yelling, mostly to the sky but also at Jaxon:

"Why am I still here?"

I was ready to hurl my bike into the bushes, storm back to the house, pack my things, and leave. I'd done my job. I'd supported every teary contestant who cried about not getting enough time with Mr. Asshole. For the ones who thought they were already in love with him after two minutes of eye contact, I reminded them there were plenty of fish in the sea. I even offered to hook them up—with hot actor friends of mine.

Of course, they didn't air that part.

Some of the women even asked why I was still there if I had no feelings for Jaxon. Barbara, the show's fixer, snapped at me:

"It's not good when the other women don't believe you like him. Convince them."

So I did.

I changed my tune, said things like, "He's okay," or "He can be nice when he wants to be."

But on the day of my meltdown on that bike trail, something weird happened.

I turned to Jaxon, voice shaking, and asked him directly: Why do you keep picking me?

He just stared at me.

Blank. Like a deer in headlights.

It was odd, because that was his chance to say something smug, call me sticky fingers again, maybe even admit he was keeping me around to torture me.

But he said nothing.

And now, after six hours of watching the show play out like it's a romantic comedy starring two people who barely tolerated each other in real life, I'm starting to wonder...

Did he know from day one?

Did he plan to kiss all the other girls, lead them on, make them swoon—only to pick me in the end? Knowing he'd never have to actually date me? Or any of them?

Was I the final twist in his fake fairytale?

"That's it."

I crawl across my bed to retrieve the remote from where I last threw it.

He knew.

He never meant to pick any of those women. Never intended to date them. Never wanted to fall in love. He played with all of their hearts—for sport.

And mine, for spectacle.

Tomorrow—no, today, technically, since it's already after midnight—I'm going to give him an earful.

SEVEN

6 HOURS LATER

I didn't even *try* to sleep until 3:00 a.m.

The meeting is at nine.

I was seventeen minutes late getting out of the car.

I'm exhausted—so much so I can barely remember the drive from Encino. Only that traffic sucked. But stopping and going, narrowly avoiding collisions… that's second nature now. I've lived in the county for more than ten years. I'm a pro at navigating arguably some the worst traffic in the world.

Before leaving, I chugged three cappuccinos because I *need* to be on my game. I have questions. Concerns. And Anne needs to answer them, put my mind at ease.

Is what they did even legal?

I signed the contract without reading it thoroughly. Anne rushed me, and I was desperate. She promised the terms were standard: I'd be paid handsomely, no nudity, no sex, and I could terminate my participation if I ever felt unsafe.

So technically... this is on me.

They used what was obviously *very good* AI to depict me falling blissfully in love with a man I *revile*. And I might've signed off on it.

Still, I've been thinking. I have a few tricks up my sleeve.

I'm running through the options in my head when the parking garage elevator doors open.

And there he is.

I jump slightly, surprised to be staring into the eyes of the last person I want to see right now.

The world stands still as we stand here, staring. I don't know what to do next. I don't want to get trapped in an elevator with him. But... God, he looks good.

Black athletic pants. Matching jacket. He's clean. Fresh. Not a trace of worry or exhaustion on his face. Meanwhile, I look—and feel—like I've been dragged through a cyclone.

"You're going up," he says. It's not a question. It's an order.

That bossy tone of his is like nails on a chalkboard. I almost tell him I'll take the next elevator—but I need him soft today. I need him pliable. He has to go along with my plan, and if I put him in combative mode, then he'll push back.

So I say nothing. I step in and take a position as far from him as possible.

Of course, he doesn't move.

No, he *plants* himself dead center, like the elevator's his personal stage.

Asshole. I really don't like this guy.

He's so unaware. So smug.

The longer I stand here, the more his presence bothers me. So, to push him back, I fake a coughing fit. Loud. Uncovered. I don't know much about athletes, but I'm pretty sure they're obsessive about their health.

"How's it been going?" he asks, entirely unbothered.

There's a smirk. Barely perceptible—but I see it. He knows I'm faking.

I give up the ruse with a sigh. "Did you watch the show?" I ask abruptly.

He looks ahead. "Yeah."

I wait. But apparently, that's all he has to say.

"What did you think?" I press.

He shrugs. "That guy really liked you."

I chuckle despite myself. "That girl really liked you."

Then I tilt my head. "But... come on."

His brown eyes cut to me—sharp. Like he has no idea what I'm talking about.

"I don't like you, Jaxon. And you don't like me. So what the hell are they doing?"

He sighs like he's deflating—letting every ounce of air drain from that tall, lean, perfectly sculpted body.

The elevator dings.

"It's just a show, Zara," he says, stepping aside to let me exit first.

I take the hint and step out. "Yeah, but it's a *fake* show. Aren't you..."

I search for the word, too tired to come up with the perfect one.

"Offended," Jaxon supplies, walking beside me.

"Yes," I say, relieved he gets it. "Offended."

At the receptionist desk, a very pretty, very thin, very *young* woman shoots to her feet like she's just been told to stand for royalty. I've seen this type a dozen times since signing with the agency. Turnover's high. Faces blur.

"They're here," she chirps into the phone. I presume she's talking to Anne.

"I mean, are we just going to let them get away with this?" I whisper to Jaxon, now that I've got him on the ropes.

The door to the agents' offices opens immediately. Another young woman—nearly a carbon copy of the receptionist—appears and gestures to us.

"Follow me." She's curt, like she's projecting Anne's irritation that we're late.

Jaxon steps off ahead of me, keeping pace with our escort. He walks tall, steady, like he has zero intention of stopping to hash anything out with me.

I sigh, nerves buzzing under my skin. I *wish* I could get a better read on him.

Still, according to the report Anne sent a few weeks ago, my reputation is back on track, my dignity somewhat restored, and all that's left is to put this absurd show behind me for good.

Jaxon and I will part ways. He'll go off with one of the girls from the cast. I'll film *Next In Line*, reclaim my career, and move the hell on.

Happy endings all around.

And honestly? I really do think Jaxon will be on board with my proposal.

So I quicken my pace to catch up with them, fairly assured that today will be the last day I ever lay eyes on Jaxon Wilde.

And then—finally—my life will be back on track.

EIGHT

"Y̲ou're late," says a man who's nearly the same height and build as Jaxon. He's older —mid-to-late forties, I'd guess—and has the air of someone who used to be an athlete himself.

I don't know why I expected Jaxon's agent to be an entertainment guy, like mine. Maybe because I keep forgetting that Jaxon and I are from completely different worlds. Eons apart, actually. If it weren't for that show, I would've never crossed paths with him.

Jaxon takes a seat on the long leather sofa. "Traffic," he says.

The man folds his arms across his chest—broad, muscular, still clearly in shape. "Aren't you at the W in Westwood? That's practically down the street."

They glare at each other.

I watch, quietly intrigued. There's a crackle of distrust in the air. His agent—at least I assume that's

37

who he is—seems to be silently asking Jaxon a question, trying to read the answer in his face.

"Okay, let's get down to business," Anne says, stepping in, all authority.

She looks far more put-together than the last time I saw her—sleek black skirt suit, tailored to perfection. It's her power uniform. Probably cost a couple grand.

I'm relieved to see her like this again. Sharp. Focused. Confident. The Anne I know. The Anne who fixes things.

And I know... it's now or never.

"I saw the show," I say, settling onto the opposite end of the sofa from Jaxon. "None of it's real."

I paste on a fake, condescending smile. "But that's okay. I must've signed something that said it was perfectly legal to turn me into a walking AI girlfriend for the sake of that dumb show. But I've been thinking —it's not too late to turn this around."

I sit up straighter. "I watched all the available episodes, tracked the girls, and I think there are a few really good options for Jaxon—"

Anne presses her fingertips to her temples. "Zara, be quiet."

My mouth stays open. I have so much more to say.

Anne flops into her oversized black office chair—it looks like a sleek ergonomic throne. "You are the winner, Zara."

I look helplessly at Jaxon, who's doing a great job

avoiding eye contact. Surely, *he* doesn't want this either.

"Wait—" I raise a hand, trying to stop this train from leaving the station. "Jaxon, did you really want to choose me? You had so much chemistry with Ashley and Heather."

He shakes his head like I'm being wildly inappropriate.

"Or…" I push on. "Is picking me your way of getting out of this as a single man? Because I don't love you, and I never will."

"Same," he snaps. But it comes out low—almost a guttural roar.

Anne claps her hands together. "So, Roger—six months. They'll do press. And in two days, the reunion."

"No." I shake my head vigorously.

"Yes, Zara. Or…" Anne closes her eyes and scratches her forehead. "Find yourself another agent."

When she opens her eyes, her expression is calm —but there's something pained in it.

My body feels light. My head tight.

Anne has never said that to me before.

"Sorry, Zara. You're pushing me to my limit. You're a great actress. You could be *big*. I still believe that. But why the hell did you shoplift?"

She jabs a finger upward, toward the ceiling. "The camera was right there. You *saw* it. I saw you look at it. And you *still* took that five-dollar face cream."

She takes a breath. Steadies herself.

I have never felt so embarrassed in my life.

And she's right. I haven't had the right attitude. People love you when you're up. But one small mistake, and they come at you with pitchforks and ridicule.

"Sorry," I say quietly. My voice cuts through the silence like glass. "You're right."

I sink deeper into the corner of the sofa, refusing to look at Jaxon—who, to his credit, is staying very quiet.

"Let's go ahead and even the score—make Zara more at ease here. Should we do it now?" the man finally says, dropping into one of the armchairs. I still don't know his name.

"What do you mean, 'even the score'?" Jaxon asks, suddenly finding his voice.

"You know her demons." Roger focuses on Anne. "She deserves to know his."

"No. No, no, no…" Jaxon mutters, shifting uncomfortably. "Not here. Not now."

"Agreed," Anne says.

It's strange how in sync she and this man are. As if they've sketched this out in advance.

The man turns to me, calm and clear. "I'm Roger Gordon. PR manager for the San Diego Bull Sharks."

I arch a brow and glance at Jaxon, jabbing my thumb toward him. "He's got demons?"

Roger raises an eyebrow. "Ever heard of *Hunks of Junk Jocks*?"

I snap my attention back to Jaxon, who's now shaking his head slowly. I see it—the faint rose blooming beneath his skin, the short, jagged breaths.

I'm about to learn his soft spot.

Something he's just as ashamed of as I am of that stupid face cream.

NINE

They don't have to tell me.

They show me.

On an iPad.

Hunks of Junk Jocks is a website exposing professional athletes accused of mistreating women. Post after post—some with photos, some with long captions—details Jaxon Wilde's alleged misdeeds. Lying. Ghosting. Using his status to lure women into bed. Screwing them, then vanishing. Fifteen of them even say he gave them the clap.

"So... did you give them the clap?" I ask, recoiling at the thought.

"No," Jaxon replies, defensive.

I study his eyes, trying to figure out if he's lying. I can't tell. But then I remember something, and shrug. "You know what? I don't care. You're a hypocrite, though. Remember what you said to me during our first meeting?" I nod, slow and righteous. "Hypocrite. A real one."

Jaxon scoots forward on the couch. "I apologized for that."

I tilt my head. "Did you mean it, though?"

"I wouldn't have said it if I didn't."

I raise a finger. "But. You flirted with nearly every woman on that show."

"To be fair, that was his job," Roger interjects.

Jaxon points at me. "Exactly. It was part of the role."

"But you *made out* with almost everyone," I snap. "I think I'm the only one who kept my distance from your mouth."

"Your choice, not mine."

I jerk back at that. Stalled.

That was a comeback I didn't see coming.

"And," Jaxon adds, "I've been tested for everything. The clap included. I'm clean. Always have been."

He says it firmly, like it's the one thing he needs me to believe. And maybe I do. Maybe.

I only look away when Anne claps her hands together, loudly. "I've got another meeting. Now that you both know why you need each other, let's wrap this up."

My head's spinning as Roger and Anne volley ideas back and forth, totally in control of the two tools in the room—Jaxon and me.

"Six months and, let's say... seven days," Anne says, sinking back into her sleek chair like the queenpin she is. "You know. Keep 'em on their toes."

"Half a year?" I squeak.

"In two days, we tape the reunion," Roger cuts in, talking right over me. "You two need to look in love."

"Understand," Anne says, "we've seen the post-show surveys. There are a lot of unhappy ladies. So the stage is going to be hot."

"But they're all under NDA," Roger adds.

"They'll still try to get under your skin," Anne warns, eyes darting between us. "They're crafty. Season after season, same story. They'll want you to crack. To expose yourselves."

I think I nod. I'm not sure. I'm too busy reeling.

This is more than learning lines. More than acting.

This is performance... but with a script I never wrote.

And God help me, I *never* wrote that I was in love with Jaxon.

"This is too much," Jaxon says, finally pushing back. "You're laying a lot on us. Why not cancel the reunion? Say I'm in training camp. Or just send one of us."

I slap my chest. "Me? You want *me* in front of the firing squad?"

"No," he says, quieter now. "But you can handle them. You're strong."

I pause, surprised.

That's twice now he's said something almost… complimentary.

"You *both* will be there," Roger snaps, commanding. "And speaking of next season—you," he points at me, "will attend every home game. But don't worry. They'll never make the playoffs."

He winks at Jaxon.

Jaxon flips him off.

"Ooh, fire in the belly. Maybe they will," Roger taunts.

"Okay, boys," Anne says, standing abruptly. "This is not a locker room. Or whatever man-space you all hype each other up in."

She checks her smartwatch. "It's set. Sadie will send your schedules. You both have my direct line— use it only if you must. Now…" She gestures toward the couch.

"Stand."

We rise.

"Show up on time for whatever's on your schedules," she finishes. "Don't be late. Don't be absent. And for God's sake—look in love."

TEN

For some reason, I feel like I just ran five miles and then spent two hours weight training in preparation for the biggest role of my life.

That's what that meeting did to me.

I barely notice that Jaxon and I are alone in the private elevator, gliding nonstop to the parking garage.

He's quiet, too. I think we're both wrung out from what just happened upstairs.

I can hardly believe this is my life right now.

This is *not* what I signed up for.

And now, in just two days, I have to face all those women from the show—women I'm *prohibited* from telling the truth. But they'll see through the lies. They *have* to. The editing was obvious. They were there. They saw how I felt—or didn't feel—about Jaxon. They'll know the producers, Anne, and Jaxon's PR guy had their hands all over every "choice." Even that final, ridiculous scene where he picked me.

Sure, the viewers bought the fairytale. But the cast?

They lived the backstage chaos.

They'll know.

"Hey."

Jaxon's voice breaks our silence, and my body tenses like I've been zapped.

Why couldn't he just stay quiet?

"Did you really look at the camera before you took… whatever you took?"

I whip my head toward him, glare sharp as glass.

"I felt like nothing more than a sex object," I say coolly, paraphrasing one of the women from *Hunks of Junk Jocks*. "After he got off, he said 'thank you,' threw on his clothes, and dropped a hundred dollars on the floor like I was a common prostitute. Is that true?"

His expression doesn't flicker. He's not smirking like usual.

Just staring—blank, unreadable.

"No," he finally says. "That's not true." His tone is low. Steady. Almost… earnest.

I lean back against the elevator wall, taking in this *new* version of Jaxon Wilde.

"This," I say, gesturing to his face. "What is *this*?"

"What's what?"

"This," I repeat, flicking my fingers toward his infuriatingly handsome face. Especially *today*. Why does he look even better outside of filming? Life isn't fair.

"What do you mean by 'this'?" he asks, genuinely confused.

His gaze stays fixed on me, unwavering, like he's trying to see something in me. I think he's trying to make me fill the silence, tell him what he wants to know.

"You know what?" I finally say. "We're not friends. Or lovers. So you don't get an answer to questions like that."

The elevator dings.

Just like earlier, Jaxon steps to the threshold and presses a hand to the door, holding it open for me. He does it casually. Almost thoughtlessly.

Is this chivalry? *Seriously?*

"Questions like what?" he asks as I pass.

I almost stop. Almost answer.

But I don't want to talk about it. Not to him. Not to anyone.

I haven't even told Anne why I did it.

Hell, I don't even know why I do it. That wasn't the first time.

I *can* explain the rush, though.

Will they let me get away with it? Is anyone even watching?

I hadn't done it again after that girl in the drugstore caught me. She made a *huge* deal about it. I offered to pay, made up some BS excuse.

She looked me dead in the eye and said:

"Bullshit!"

So angry, that one.

So smug. So *righteous*.

She'd caught a once-rising actress on her little hook, and she wasn't about to throw me back into the ocean. Not a chance.

But that's a lot to explain. Especially to a guy I can't stand.

A guy who's also… one huge, maddening enigma.

I keep walking.

But at least I raise my hand behind me and say, "Bye."

ENGINE IDLING, I SIT IN THE DRIVER'S SEAT OF MY car, fingers clamped around the steering wheel like it's the only thing keeping me upright. I feel so...

What are the words?

Ding, dum, ding...

I glance at the name flashing across the dash and press *Answer*.

"That was brutal," I say.

"You need me to be brutal," Anne replies without missing a beat. "Your career depends on it. And don't forget to thank me when you're holding that Best Lead Actress trophy for *Next In Line*."

There's a pause. Then her voice softens, just enough.

"But yeah… as your friend, I was a bitch." A sigh. "I'll make it up to you. Come to dinner tonight? You've been holed up in that house too long. Not just hiding — disappearing. That's not healthy, Zara. You need people. You need air. It's time to come back to the real world, okay?"

I bite down on the back of my teeth and clutch the wheel tighter. Anne knows me too well. She knows I haven't been living healthily since the show ended— knows exactly what I'm prone to become when the noise dies down. And I want that. God, I want it so badly. The silence. The slipping away. But it's not good for me. I will lose everything if I give in to that part of myself.

So, I gut it up, force the words out, and say,

"What time?"

ELEVEN

Anne lives in Bel-Air with her husband, Rich Conway—a mega-producer and a major reason her clients land the best roles. I was lucky to land her as my agent.

By the time I reach the gated community, I'm frazzled from traffic. God, I hate driving in this city. It would've been a nightmare if I didn't know the back streets. In L.A., those who master the side routes win the war. And thankfully, I know my way around.

Anne and Rich's home is modest by Bel-Air standards. A Spanish-style, white-stone two-story tucked behind towering hedges, framed by blooming jacaranda trees that look like lavender clouds. It's tasteful. Quiet. Like they're hiding from the industry that made them.

A housekeeper leads me through a cool, open foyer, where a tall olive tree stands beneath a skylight.

My entire place in Encino could fit inside their first floor. But it still feels cozy. Every piece is curated without being pretentious—soft beige walls, pale oak floors, and art chosen with taste, not just money. A massive black-and-white portrait of Eartha Kitt winks at me from above a console table. That feels like Anne.

We pass through a sunken living room: cream sofas, a faded Moroccan rug, books stacked like sculpture. A fireplace that looks unused. The air smells faintly of eucalyptus and something herbal—like Anne has her own candle line she's keeping secret.

Floor-to-ceiling sliding doors are open to the backyard. The ocean breeze drifts in, light and warm. I really have to think about moving out of the Valley. It's blazing hot at my place. The A/C never turns off.

Outside, under a wide veranda wrapped in flowering vines, a cozy wooden table is set for dinner. String lights hang in soft lines overhead.

Anne is already there, barefoot, in linen pants and a sleeveless white eyelet top, wine in hand, looking like her day just exhaled.

"You made it!" she says, pouring me a glass from the chilled bottle.

I raise my hands, wiggling my fingers. "I have."

"Good." She hands me the glass. "Sit. Rich had a new brick pizza oven installed. We're having his famous loaded pizza. You'll love it."

"Right," I say cautiously. "You're talking fast. Am I still in trouble?"

"Remember how we met?" she asks, skipping right past my question.

And just like that, my mind drifts back to one of the most pivotal nights of my life.

We met by accident. I was working a catering gig in Holmby Hills. The uniform was black, A-line, and way too short. The top plunged so low I spent most of the night terrified a boob would pop out. I hated the job, but I needed the money. Rent was due. My fridge was empty. I'd missed minimum payments on all five credit cards.

Yes—I was sexualizing myself for the paycheck. But I was there to serve food, not the jerk who cornered me during a bathroom break, shoved me against the wall, and tried to pull my panties down.

It happened fast. One second I was pinned—the next, I heard a splat. His eyes rolled back, and he hit the floor.

There stood all five feet, two inches of Anne Park, holding a full glass water bottle like a weapon.

"He'll live," she said, coolly.

"I could've handled it," I mumbled.

"I'm sure you could. But it won't ruin my career," she said. Then, cocking an eyebrow, "Let me guess— you're an actress?"

Of course she was right. The man she clocked was powerful. But Rich was more powerful.

When I asked how she knew what was about to happen, I'll never forget her reply:

"He'd been watching you all night. He's done this before. Three women tried to report him. He denied it every time. I had a feeling he'd try again. So I waited."

She saved my career that night. I would've fought back. That's my red line. I don't sleep with anyone—or let anyone take advantage of me—for a part.

While he groaned on the floor, Anne explained everything to security. He didn't press charges. Didn't even look at me. Just slithered out.

Then she turned to me and asked, "Do you have a job?"

"Yeah. I have to get back to work."

"No. An acting job."

"Not yet."

That's when she handed me an audition. Said if I booked it, she'd represent me. It was for Agent Laura Merton on the primetime drama *Emergency*.

I booked it.

From that moment on, my life changed. I never thought I'd make it in this city. Not really. I thought I'd crawl back to Indio, defeated. But I didn't. All thanks to Anne.

And so, to answer her question now, I say, "I'll never forget it."

She pats her chest. "Me neither. When I saw you, I thought: This girl has the it factor. But can she act?

Then you booked that role, out of the gate. You've gone further, faster than any of my clients. So why are you self-sabotaging?"

"I'm not," I say, sealing the weak denial with a sip of wine.

Anne shakes her head. "Roger's worried. He thinks you're a risk to Jaxon's career. That's why, after you left, he pulled Jaxon from the deal. That's why I invited you here."

My heart drops into my stomach.

"But," she says—and I love her 'buts'—"he called back after my meeting. Right before I phoned Jan Marshall, who's producing *Next In Line*. Your spot is still *contingent* on your public image staying intact."

"What did Roger say?" I ask, now leaning forward.

"Jaxon's back in. Barely. You need him more than he needs you. According to the focus group, he'd be out of the doghouse if he'd picked Ashley—who, by the way, is still an option."

I deflate. "Why didn't he pick her? That would've worked better for both of us."

Anne twists her mouth. She does that when she's weighing her words.

"Truth?"

"Truth."

"He didn't want to commit to any of them. That's what made you the perfect choice."

"His commitment issues aren't my problem."

Anne tilts her head. Then slowly sits back and takes another sip of wine.

"What?" I ask, seeing the look on her face. "I'm the problem?"

She snorts. "*You* are the problem, Zara. I've tried to wrap my head around this. I don't think you feel remorse for what you did—or any real appreciation for what I did for you. If he'd sent you home in week one, that would've been it. You were rude. Entitled. Oblivious to how dire things were. So no, it's not just a *him* problem. You're his problem. You're *my* problem. And frankly, you're your own problem. So get it together." She points at me. "I love you, but if you mess this up—I'm done."

"Dinner's ready!" Rich announces, appearing with a giant pizza balanced on one hand. The smell is divine. My stomach turns anyway.

"Oh," he says, catching the tension.

"I know I made it hard," I mutter. "I didn't want to fight him. I wanted to like him. But…" I drop my head. "I'm sorry. I'll do better."

"Good!" Anne lights up. "That's all I ask. And you better, *do better*."

TWELVE

REUNION DAY

8:00 A.M.

I spent most of yesterday in bed, haunted by Anne's warning. If she drops me, no one else will pick me up. I'm sure of it.

There was a time when half the agents in town tried to woo me away from her. Not anymore. I'm damaged goods. And yesterday, I let myself wallow in that truth.

Today, I arrived at least fifteen minutes before my 8 a.m. call time. I need Anne to *see* that I'm taking this seriously. I believe her when she says she'll drop me. She's my agent, yes—but more than that, she's arguably my best friend. And I get it now. I took our bond for granted.

So, I've been repeating a mantra. It's still looping in my head as hair and makeup prep me for the stage.

Do your job. Take the emotion out. No matter what, be professional. This is the new role of your life.

"Oh, I forgot to tell you—congratulations," Janet chirps. She's the same makeup artist from the shoot. "Jaxon Wilde is hot as hell. So..." She flicks her eyebrows. "How's the sex?"

"It's great," I say, singing it like a Broadway lead. Too much. But I'm already in character.

She freezes, narrowing her eyes to inspect my face.

I pour it on thick—eyes wide, lips curled, like I've just remembered something steamy. "So, so, so good."

In reality, I'd bet money he's terrible in bed. He's not nearly eager enough to please a woman.

"Yeah?" she says, clearly thrilled by the idea of Jaxon as a sex god.

"Yeah." I grin, lying through my teeth.

She tilts her head thoughtfully. "Funny, though. I could've sworn you hated him."

"I did. Initially." *(Chuckle sweetly. Nostalgic tone.)* "He grew on me."

"Awwww," she coos, practically swooning. "So you've been undercover lovers since filming ended? Tonight you can finally come out as a real couple in real life. That has to be exciting."

The silence blooms—expectant. She's waiting for more. For something juicy.

I want to sigh. Loudly. I want to beg her to just shut up and finish making me look human. But...

Do your job. Take the emotion out. No matter what. Be professional. This is the new role of your life.

"I can hardly wait for the whole world to see us in love," I say, my voice syrupy. "Because we are. Sooo in love."

A laugh slips out. I sound ridiculous even to myself.

Thankfully, Janet doesn't catch the irony.

"I've worked on this show for five seasons, and not one of the couples lasted more than six months. But I think *you two*? You'll go the distance. Right, Missie?"

Missie—the hairdresser—stays quiet.

I glance over.

Her eyes are exaggeratedly wide. Wide enough to say everything she won't out loud.

They know.

Everyone believes we're a sham.

And they're right.

But when I walk out on that stage, it's my and Jaxon's job to convince them not to believe their lying eyes, but to believe *us*—the two liars.

Ugh.

I hate that I have to do this.

THIRTEEN

2 HOURS LATER

First of all, I can't say I'm baffled by what I'm watching unfold on camera.

According to Anne, Jaxon never even wanted to pick Ashley. He thought she was clingy. *Clingy*. But look at him now—pretending she's so precious. Holding her hand, gazing at her like she's a fallen star. The way he plays it, the world will think he didn't choose her *because she was too good for him*.

And before Ashley even took the stage—red-faced and freshly tear-streaked—the other girls had already let him off the hook.

"He did not see the part of Zara that we saw," Aimee, one of the more desperate cast members, said with theatrical resignation. "And that's all I'm saying."

One girl after another stood up to accuse *me*.

Saying I played both sides. That I told them one thing and told Jaxon another. That I wasn't honest about my feelings. But then—just to keep their hands clean—they'd close their comments with lines like:

"But if they're *really* in love, then I'm happy for them."

Anne warned me last night how brutal this day would be. "They're all under NDA," she reminded me. "So… remember that."

I'm repeating my mantra, trying to stay centered, but the words start crashing into each other like bumper cars. I'm losing my grip.

Do your job. Take the emotion out. Be professional.

This is the role. This is the role. This is the—

Ashley breathes in deeply, shoulders rising like she's about to sing a solo at the talent show.

"If you're in love with her," she says in her soft, princessy voice, "then who am I to get in the way?"

The crowd of women—the audience, the cast, the fairytale believers—erupt into applause like she's just sacrificed her heart on a velvet altar.

I don't need a teleprompter to know: I'm the villain.

I know it the moment Dave Lyons, the host, turns back to the camera and says:

"Well, we'll hear from Jaxon's *controversial pick* when we return. But first, let's relive Jaxon and Zara's breathtaking journey of love."

"Ready Zara to enter stage right," I hear in my ear.

FINALLY, I TAKE MY SEAT.

In the audience, all eyes are on me. Expressions are somber. Tension thickens the air like fog. My survival instincts switch to high alert. I get it—the viewing audience feels duped. And based on what they've heard so far, I'm not a "girl's girl," no matter how production painted me.

"Are you okay?" Jaxon's voice interrupts the mantra looping in my head.

I nod—barely.

We're sitting too close on this faux-romantic loveseat. We were instructed to snuggle up, to let the world *see* how much we love each other. Only now do I realize how much unconscious refuge I've taken in the heat of his arm pressed against mine, and his thigh—tense, tight, and hollow—against my leg.

"Don't worry, I've got your back," he says softly.

I scoot half an inch away.

Across from us, Ashley sits in the single chair—the exile seat. Frankly, I don't like what this setup implies *any more than she does*. No matter what Anne said about Jaxon not really being into her, that's not what I saw. That's not what any of the girls saw. She *should* be in my seat. That's what her glare says. That's what this whole room says.

"This is so terrible," I whisper. "Why did you even make her think she had a chance when…" I trail off, turning toward Jaxon and letting my expression finish the question.

Our eyes meet. Have I *ever* sat this close to him in real life?

Sure, the show used whatever magic it needed—AI, editing, maybe even a little puppeteering—to manufacture intimacy. But this? *This* feels new.

I smell his minty breath. His lips look softer than I remember. Have I ever noticed them before? Why am I noticing them *now*?

"I know," he says.

My brows shoot up.

Then higher still when he adds, "I should've thought better."

"Everybody take your places," the floor director calls out.

Our first meeting flashes through my mind. The awkward dates. The night he had dinner delivered to his room like he was over it before it started. The kisses he gave to nearly every woman like they belonged to him. It all rushes back.

Don't fall for whatever act he's putting on now, I warn myself.

But I lean into it anyway, using it as a moment to strengthen my character. I gaze at his objectively handsome face, bat my lashes, and grin like a boy-crazy teenager. He meets me halfway with a sensual smirk.

Good for him. I'm one hundred percent convinced Jaxon should've been an actor instead of a football player.

We hold the look just long enough to sell the illusion.

Then, from his host's seat, Dave Lyons' smooth, affable voice—*the only kind that could sell this much bullshit and still sound charming*—calls my name.

Showtime.

FOURTEEN

"How are you feeling, finally being able to let the world know you're a couple?" Dave asks, right after saying my name.

This is one of the questions I *did* prepare for.

"It's a huge relief," I say, leaning my shoulder into Jaxon's as he stretches his arm across the back of our plush purple velvet love seat. "Keeping the secret has been hard. We had to sneak around just to be together. But now? We're here. Out in the open."

I turn to Jaxon, bat my lashes, hold eye contact for three seconds—just like I practiced—and then shift my gaze back to Dave.

"What do you say to the other women who question the authenticity of your relationship?"

"I say…" Jaxon jumps in before I can get a word out. I had a whole answer rehearsed for that one, too. "I went with my heart and my gut. Choosing Zara wasn't easy. I never wanted to hurt anyone. But if I hadn't been interested in her, she never would've made it to the final pinning."

I exhale—just slightly—relieved he's doing what he promised: having my back.

"Well, that's surprising to me," Ashley cuts in, her Disney-princess voice sharp and rising. "Because Zara never said she had any interest in him. At all."

"Actually, she said the opposite," Heather chimes in from the front row of contestants.

"Same," adds Marie, raising a finger like she's in class.

"I don't know how she went from constantly calling him a 'dingbat with abs' to saying yes to the final pen," Sara says.

I open my mouth, but nothing comes out. And worse—Jaxon has removed his arm from the back of the couch. The signal is clear. He's not protecting me anymore.

"I don't remember calling him a dingbat," I say, weakly. Which is a lie, because now that they've said it, I *do* remember. I did call him that. Because, well... he kind of is.

"And she didn't even want to be there," another girl piles on.

"Now she's lying," Ashley says, taking over like she's the spokesperson for Team Morality. "She used to say all the time that he was all abs and no brain. And hey—if that was her opinion, fine. But I'm thinking about him and who's right for him, and honestly? It's not her."

I glance at Jaxon. He leans away from me. His jaw is tight, clenched. *Really?* He's shocked I didn't like him? He didn't like me either. And now he's backpedaling. *Asshole.*

"I don't know, I—" I start, stalling. I let the silence stretch, let the suspense build just long enough for the camera to catch it. "I agree with all of you," I say, finally. "Jaxon and I had a slow start. We did. Sure, we had great dates, great debates, and great conversations whenever we stole time together, as you all saw… But I honestly don't remember referring to him as a dingbat. He's a very successful quarterback—"

"Wide receiver," Jaxon corrects in a low, gritted voice.

"Right!" I say brightly, slapping my forehead. "Wide receiver. But I was going to say… I made personal relationships with all of you, and I would've been happy for any one of you if Jaxon had chosen you."

I place my hand gently on his knee, a small gesture of claim. He doesn't put his hand over mine.

"But he chose me. And I chose him. We're falling in love more and more every day, learning from each other, loving each other. He's *certainly* not a dingbat. And my heart…" I summon tears to the edges of my eyes, and they come on cue. "My heart is open—still and forever—to every single one of you. Because I could've walked away from this with nothing but the friendships I made in the house, and still felt like I won."

I'm shivering a little, because—if I'm being honest—I *meant* the last part. Or I used to. Now? After they just tried to throw me under the bus like that?

Bitches.

But at least the audience is eating it up. They're applauding. Some are even dabbing at their eyes. My performance has landed.

Only when I turn my teary gaze to Jaxon do I see what's behind *his* eyes—and I swear, I've scared the hell out of him.

He's looking at me like I'm a stranger. Like I'm a liar. Like I'm some kind of beautiful, soulless machine.

And maybe I am. I hate this feeling. I want to tell him this was survival. That I had to fight, claw, and *perform* to protect us both.

But the truth is, he faltered. He pulled back. I had to carry us.

And I *will* let him know it.

FIFTEEN

All the girls must've gotten their warning to halt assassinating my character. The fake smiles plastered across their faces say it all. Suddenly, everyone wishes us the best. Says they're happy for our "happily ever after."

Not one of them says they want to be my friend. *Whatever*.

Thankfully, Jaxon and I are the final scene of the show. To bring the season to its glittery end, balloons, confetti, and—ugh, what is this sticky crap?—glitter rain down from the ceiling.

"Kiss him!" Betty yells in my ear, still producing my every last moment. I can't wait to never hear her voice again.

Jaxon must've gotten the same direction because he wraps an arm around my waist. But instead of kissing me, he leans in, lips brushing my ear.

"Dingbat? You think I'm a dingbat?" he whispers.

Gleefully—like I'm genuinely thrilled by the sparkly garbage falling on me—I rise on my tiptoes, lean close to his ear (he's *so* tall), and say, "Let's talk after this."

His large hands grip my waist.

"Where?" he murmurs.

When he lifts me off the floor and spins me around for the cameras, I feel light as air.

"My dressing room," I whisper back, lips grazing his ear.

And... damn it. That does something to me. Down *there*. Something I have absolutely no intention of acknowledging. Just biology. Nothing more.

"Okay," he says, lowering me back to the stage.

He doesn't exactly give me a soft landing. *Asshole.*

"And cut!" the director calls.

Jaxon grabs my hand and all but hauls me offstage. His grip is hot, urgent. Everyone watches, stunned—especially the producers—as we slip through the dark hallways.

My heart hammers until I finally get the door to my dressing room open.

"Tanya, Missie, could you give us a second?" I ask my hair and makeup artists.

They exchange another one of those *raised-eyebrow* looks, but thankfully, they leave.

Now we're alone.

"What the hell was that? You said nothing as they

attacked me. I thought you had my back," I snap, pointing a thumb back toward the stage.

"Dingbat? Really?" Jaxon growls. "You called me a dingbat?"

I sigh and close my eyes, trying not to lose it.

"I can't believe you're harping on that."

He's staring at me like I'm the one who's lost her mind. Maybe I am. But that doesn't mean I'm wrong.

"I don't know," I say, trying to defuse the situation. We have the better part of six months to pretend we like each other, so I can't have him hating me even more already. "You must've done some... dingbat thing, which is why I said it. But..."

"You don't even know me," he snaps. "You never tried to. And you've been rude since day one."

"Ha!" I scoff. "*Me*? You've been rude. What did you call me—Sticky Fingers? Mocking my..."

I stop. I can't say *my crime*. The shame still catches in my throat.

"I apologized for that," he says, and I'm shocked into silence. Because if he hadn't said anything, he would've had me beat right there, leaving me drowning in the humiliation of what I had done. "You don't know how to let things go."

I cross my arms and plant my feet. "Says the guy still mad I called him a dingbat."

"And all that crying, shaky voice—was that an act? Because you're *way* too good at lying."

I jab a finger into my own chest, stepping closer.

75

"I was saving our asses," I hiss. "While you sat there sulking. Haven't you been called worse? Dingbat, dingbat, dingbat!"

We lock eyes, breathing hard.

And then it happens. That *thing*.

The tension thickens. The air shifts. Something warm and heavy pulses between us. Something neither of us is ready to name.

He licks his bottom lip slowly, draws it into his mouth, and I swear I feel it in every cell of my body.

Then—*knock knock knock.*

"Jaxon, we gotta go!" a voice calls from the hallway.

Jaxon steps back. Shakes his head. Turns his back on me.

And just like that, it's over.

Once the door clicks shut, I stagger back until my fingers find the edge of my vanity stool. I sink onto it, dazed.

"What the hell was *that*?" I whisper.

I shake my head. *Let it go. Let it go.*

I cannot be hot for the likes of Jaxon Wilde.

Not now.

Not ever.

SIXTEEN

2 MONTHS LATER

When I first got my script in hand, I walked through my house clutching the freshly bound pages, sniffing the crisp paper, and hugging them against my chest. It felt so good to be back at work. I've memorized all my lines —and all my co-stars' too. I'm so ready, it's ridiculous.

It's nighttime. I stand in front of my sliding glass doors, feeling dwarfed by the size of them. Sometimes, it's hard to believe this is my home. That I bought it myself.

My beginnings weren't just humble—they were distressing. I study the reflection staring back at me. Her eyes are solid. Mouth relaxed. She's real. I could pinch myself and feel it.

My gaze moves past the glass to the pool outside,

the aqua blue water flickering with the wind. I've made it. I have a home I love. A swimming pool. A career. I used to fantasize about this life—and now, I'm living it.

Script in hand, lines ready to be performed, I pause and ask myself: *How do I feel about me?*

Before I can answer, my phone rings, announcing Anne Park.

I rush to my desk, grab my device, and swipe to answer. Anne only calls at this hour when it's something work-related.

"Hey. Are you ready for tomorrow?" she asks.

I stiffen. *Tomorrow?* "Um…" I rush to my desktop computer and open the calendar app. I can't believe I missed something so important that Anne would call and remind me. At some point, I really need to hire an assistant.

"You don't remember?" she asks.

The date block is empty. But I click on it anyway, just in case. "If production's starting tomorrow instead of in two weeks, I'm still good. I know my—"

"No. That's not what you've forgotten, Zara."

Her voice makes me go still. Alert.

"Then, what *have* I forgotten?" I ask, pulse beginning to race.

SEVENTEEN

JAXON WILDE

GAME DAY

"Hi, Jaxon."

One of the cheerleaders wiggles her fingers at me as we line up to take the field.

I've never seen her before. She must be new. But the way she says my name—like we've got history—anyone watching probably thinks we do.

We don't.

I can't flirt with cheerleaders anymore. Those days are over.

I tilt my head back and press my fingers into my eyes, trying to reset. Zara and I were supposed to meet upstairs—get briefed on camera cues, learn when to react and where to look. That was the plan.

Instead, Roger and I sat there alone.

"I knew she'd pull this shit," he spat.

He's been pushing to swap her out with Ashley ever since the reunion.

"She's more agreeable," he said.

Translation: she's easier.

And she is. But I've always found *easy* boring—and Ashley bores me. Plus, Roger's thinking is short-sighted. You can't just swap women like jerseys after the final pinning.

So I pushed back. "We're sticking with Zara. End of story."

"You don't get to make that call. I do," he snapped.

"You mean *we* do," I said.

We glared at each other. Roger and I mostly tolerate each other. The guy's a bulldozer. I've had to play him like a fiddle—make him think my ideas are his.

"Let's just stick with the plan for now. She'll show us how we need to move forward from here," I said.

"You like her," Roger said.

"What? No."

He gave me that look. The one that calls bullshit and doesn't blink.

Yeah, Zara's complicated. And I kind of like complicated. She jumps to conclusions. She can be a pain in the ass.

But *like her*? Take her seriously as a real girlfriend? I'd be stupid to do that.

Even though she's hot as hell. Sexy—very sexy.

Smart, too. But too damn unpredictable.

Still, I thought—at the very least—she was a professional.

"I'm calling. See what the hell's going on," Roger muttered, jabbing at his phone.

She answered after the first ring.

"Where the hell are you!" he barked.

She sounded frantic. Didn't know she was on speaker. Started rambling about a last-minute fashion show fitting. Said she planned to drive to San Diego after, but traffic was brutal. So she booked a commercial flight instead.

"You booked your own flight?" Roger snapped. "You don't have an assistant?"

"No. Not yet."

"You need one. We'll get you one. Immediately. Because if this happens again—"

She promised she was boarding soon.

That was three hours ago.

Now, as we take the field—pads popping, adrenaline firing—I glance up at the suite where she's supposed to be. VIPs. The team owner. Wives. Girlfriends. Media reps.

Zara's not there.

I shake my head.

She's a trained actress. She knows what call times are. She knows how this works. If she doesn't care

81

enough to show up for me—or even for herself—what are we doing?

Maybe Roger's right. Maybe I should make a clean break. Go with Ashley. Or Heather. At this point, it's a toss-up.

If she's not in that suite by kickoff, I'm done.

I exhale hard. Slap hands with my teammates. Let my game face drop into place.

The crowd's on its feet.

"Let's go!" I roar, pumping my fist toward the stands.

Time to forget about this fucking uncomfortable feeling in my chest—and wreck Seattle.

EIGHTEEN

15 MINUTES LATER

"Oh my gosh... oh my gosh," I repeat under my breath, trailing a stadium usher who's power-walking me through endless corridors toward the suite I was supposed to be in *before* kickoff.

What a day.

Before this Jaxon Wilde situation was added to the mix, I could manage my schedule. I had a system. Now? I'm racing through a stadium, smelling like airplane air, my makeup melted down my face, my hair frizzed from the humidity rolling off the SoCal coast.

Unacceptable.

And I'm tired. So very, very tired.

"Wait," I pant, stopping abruptly in front of the ladies' room. I point to the door. "I just need to freshen up."

The usher glances at her watch, tight-lipped like I'm testing the limits of her orders to get me upstairs *now*.

"Alright, just make it quick, okay?"

I nod and rush inside.

The mirror confirms what I feared—I look like I lost a fight with a Halloween costume. So, I scrub off the makeup. Better to go barefaced than look like a trainwreck in foundation. I yank my hair into a pony-tail, then braid it. Thank God I keep body wipes and deodorant in my purse. I scrub away the airplane stench I hate so much and reapply a quick layer of fresh.

Then I *finally* pee—my bladder had been on the verge of bursting since before we landed. Between disembarking, signing autographs, and getting whisked to the stadium in the car Roger sent, I haven't had a second to breathe.

When I reemerge, my usher speaks into her walkie-talkie. "Here she is." Then, without waiting for a response, she stomps off. I follow.

When we reach the suite, Roger's standing at the door, suited up like he's about to take a deposition—and so furious I half-expect steam to shoot from his ears.

"Sorry," I say quickly, lowering my head like a school kid caught sneaking in late.

"Strike one," he hisses. Then he turns and walks off, leaving me to face the suite alone.

Everyone in the room is staring at me like I'm part of a museum exhibit.

NINETEEN

I t smells amazing in here—like sweet, expensive perfume. I'm pretty sure it's coming from all the women seated in the rows ahead of me. And definitely from the one beside me.

She's all long everything—long hair, long nails, skyscraper heels. Her pants are so tight they might as well be airbrushed on, and her strappy blouse is also painted on. She, and all the other women in this suite, are basically sex personified.

I finally look down at myself.

Baggy jeans. SoCal casual. A white V-neck tee. At least my Converse high-tops have a wedge heel. I guess I look... stylish? But for what—lunch at a beach café?

If I were sitting with the general public, I'd be dressed appropriately.

The woman next to me suddenly turns and says, "By the way, nice to finally meet you."

I'm startled. Until now, she and the rest of the suite have felt like characters in a high-budget dream sequence I wasn't cast for.

"Oh," I say, taking her small, manicured hand. Her fingers are weighed down with rings, but I clock the one that matters—her wedding band.

"I'm Genesis," she adds. "Barber Cartwright's wife."

"Um…" I nod like I know who that is. I'm pretty sure he's one of the players on the field.

Suddenly, the entire suite tenses—everyone leaning forward in their seats. Something just happened on the field. All I see are men moving in chaos. It's impossible to track. A moment later, Genesis and the others sink back, visibly disappointed.

Guess that wasn't the play they wanted.

"Anyway," she continues, running a hand through her hair and then flipping it, "my job is to show you around and introduce you to the ladies. Make you feel at home, like you fit in."

Like you fit in. I caught that. She knows I don't.

"Thank you," I say anyway.

"At the end of last season," she goes on, "every time Jaxon touched the ball, the stadium would erupt in boos. It was awful—so embarrassing for him. But today?" She brightens. "He touched the ball earlier. And it was quiet. No boos. That's because of you."

She smiles, and I notice her over-plumped lips. Why would someone do that to their face?

Still, I scramble for a line, something breezy and charming.

"Thank God we fell in love, then," I sing with fake cheer.

The second I say it, I want to kick myself. That was awful. Not even a bad reality show writer would've penned that line.

"I mean... that's actually pretty stupid," I blurt, trying to recover.

Genesis frowns, clearly wondering *why* I said that, which—ironically—means my first line might've worked better. But it's too late now. She's still looking at me, expecting more.

So I ramble. "The, uh, booing thing—just because of what a few women wrote on a website? His dating life shouldn't affect his career. That's all I meant."

I'm sweating. Stress sweat. The stinkiest kind.

Genesis leans in slightly. "No, honey," she says with a laugh, "he just needs a wife." Then she smiles wider. "And you're his boo. So—no more boos."

My mouth stays open, unsure what to say after that.

He just needs a wife?

That's crazy.

But I don't trust myself to say the *right* thing again, so instead, I raise my hand to get the attention of the waiter covering our section. I'm starving.

I order a grilled shrimp po' boy and a bottle of still water. No alcohol—not with production starting soon. No room for mistakes.

As I wait for my food, boredom starts to gnaw at me. I have no clue what's happening on the field, and I feel about as connected to this world as a background extra in a scene I didn't audition for.

"Chris is in! Look, look, look!" one of the women squeals, pointing down like she's just been put into the game too.

The energy in the suite shifts. Everyone is perched on the edge of their plush seats, locked in, emotionally invested.

"Smile…" Genesis elbows me gently. "Now, now…"

I glance up—just in time to see myself on the big screen.

My smile flashes, a second too late.

Next to Genesis, I look plain. Casual. Like a fan who wandered into the VIP section by mistake. She, of course, looks flawless.

But even as I force the smile, I can't stop my mind from spinning.

Jaxon must see this too.

What's he thinking now—seeing me like this? Dressed like this? Late, barely pulled together, on his biggest day of the season?

TWENTY

JAXON WILDE

"There she is," Barber says, nodding toward the Jumbotron as I slump onto the bench, cooling off.

I've been on the field a while. Dropped the ball once. Forced out of bounds twice to avoid getting obliterated. Chauncy Boyd's on me like white on rice —or more accurately, like flies on shit. He's got my number today.

I glance up. And there she is.

Zara.

Her face fills the screen, all lit up with a camera-ready smile. She's waving, trying hard to play the part.

She doesn't fit in up there. Not with the wives and girlfriends. Not with the polished gloss of that world.

And somehow, I like that.

She's out of place, but she's *her*.

I wonder what Ben Robinson, Jake Ness, Griff

Howes, and Cal Navarro are saying about her on the broadcast. Then, my own face shows up beside hers on the screen.

Side-by-side.

We look good together.

I've never really seen it until now. But... yeah. We do.

Then suddenly she looks away, reaching for something.

Food.

She's pulling a sandwich from a tray like she's been waiting all day to eat it. I squint. Is that a shrimp po' boy?

Genesis leans toward her, says something, probably trying to coach her into playing it up for the camera.

But Zara? Her eyes roll back like she's in heaven from the first bite. Then she gives a slow, exaggerated thumbs-up—mouth full—and the entire stadium *loses it*.

Roars of laughter and cheers.

And she's just... chewing. Like nothing happened. Like she's not being watched by seventy-thousand fans and a national audience.

"She must be hungry," Barber says, cracking up. "Is that a po' boy? Damn."

I chuckle, trying to hide it—but I can feel it. The grin pulling at my face.

Barber glances at me, smirking. "Look at you."

"What?"

"I never thought I'd see the day you'd look at a woman like that."

I shake my head, trying to wipe the smile off my face. But he's not wrong.

This is a game. I've got a job to do.

I refocus on the field.

Chauncy Boyd is waiting.

I need to shake him. I need to score.

TWENTY-ONE

A WHILE LATER

"How long does this game last?" I ask, shifting in my seat for what feels like the hundredth time. "Like, how long does it take to play one game of football? And why do they even need a halftime? Just play through. Get it over with."

Genesis turns and looks at me like I've just kicked her shin. "Honey, what is *wrong* with you?"

"I don't understand this game," I admit, loud enough for a few nearby heads to turn. I don't even care anymore.

"It's not complicated," she snaps. "One team tries to get the ball across the field. The other team tries to stop them. That's it."

Her tone stings more than it should. I instantly

regret speaking. I don't want to talk to her again— ever, if I can help it. But it's my job to keep things copacetic, to maintain this illusion of cohesion.

"Sorry," I murmur.

But she's not done. "How do you go on a show to *date* a football player and not know *anything* about what he does?"

"That was one of the show's requirements," I say flatly. "Contestants couldn't know anything about sports. It was supposed to be about emotional connection."

"Well, that's dumb," she scoffs. "That's why those relationships never last. Your man needs you to *be in the game* with him. You should breathe him, sleep him, *eat* him, honey."

"That's true," Chris's wife chimes in from the row below, pretending not to have been eavesdropping but clearly listening the whole time.

I resist the urge to argue. Even if Jaxon and I were *really* a couple, I would never base my entire life around his career. That's just not who I am. But I bite my tongue. I'm not here to make enemies or stand on a soapbox. I just need to survive this.

I reach into my purse, grab my sunglasses, and slip them on.

I just need to close my eyes for one second.

WHAT SOUNDS LIKE DISTANT THUNDER TURNS OUT TO be the crowd going *absolutely* wild. Someone's jabbing my arm. I jolt upright, catching myself before I completely collapse onto the woman next to me.

Holy crap. Did I just fall asleep?

I blink at the Jumbotron. The word **TOUCH-DOWN** is emblazoned across the screen in giant letters. Jaxon's on it—center stage, standing there, scowling… *at a replay of me.*

There I am, dead asleep. Mouth slack. Sunglasses slightly askew.

And now that I'm fully awake, I can feel it— *everyone* is staring at me. Genesis. The other wives. The camera crew. All frowning. Judging. Horrified.

I missed it. I missed Jaxon's touchdown.

Oh—no.

TWENTY-TWO

I can't leave until I see Jaxon and explain what happened.

Being caught on camera *sleeping*—during his touchdown, no less—is nothing short of a PR catastrophe. Roger's been calling nonstop. I'm sure he's tearing through the stadium like a lunatic, looking for me. But I electronically sent an usher five hundred bucks to sneak me down to the tunnels and keep me hidden from anyone with a camera or a clipboard.

I *cannot* be seen right now. Not after that.

How do I come back from this?

I'm tucked into a shadowy little alcove near the loading docks, pacing in tiny, panicked steps, when Anne's name flashes across my phone. I groan, scratching at my scalp like that'll somehow knock loose a better idea than answering.

Should I wait to talk to Jaxon first?

Is the usher even doing what I paid him to do, or did he just take my money and ghost me?

Screw it. I answer.

"Hello?" I whisper.

"What the *fuck* was that?" Anne shrieks through the speaker.

I wince. "Sorry," I say—and jump, startled by how loud my voice echoes in this cramped space. I lower it fast. "Sorry," I repeat, barely audible.

"I was tired," I murmur. "It's been a crazy day. And I don't even *understand* this stupid game."

"You *fell asleep*."

"I know."

"*During his touchdown*, Zara?"

"I know." My head drops. Shame settles in like a hundred-pound weight.

"Roger is furious. He's over it. Meeting's at ten a.m. tomorrow. No excuses."

Before I can respond, I hear a voice—male, close.

"Zara?"

I turn around. It's the usher. His face is apologetic, almost guilty.

"Sorry," he says. "He won't come. I'll send your money back."

I shake my head, heart sinking. "No. It's okay. I'll see him tomorrow."

And that's it. No chance to explain. No shot to fix it.

Just silence—and the crushing weight of it.

My goose? Cooked. Charred. Fried. Already scraped off the plate and dumped in the trash.

THE USHER'S NAME IS RAY, AND HE EARNS EVERY CENT I paid him. He guides me out of the stadium and onto a busy San Diego street without a single person spotting me.

It's nighttime now. People are out—laughing, eating, living their lives. Meanwhile, I'm spiraling from a PR nightmare and no clean way home.

I don't have my car. I could rent one and drive back to L.A., drop it off there. Amtrak's an option, but I'll get recognized just as easily as I would at the airport.

So I make a bold choice.

I call Anne back.

I tell her the truth: I'm stuck in San Diego, and I need help.

And to her credit, Anne gives me exactly what I ask for.

TWENTY-THREE

JAXON WILDE

"It's cool, Jax," Micah, our quarterback, says. "It makes perfect sense. She ate, her blood sugar spiked, she got sleepy. Biology, man." He claps me on the back. "Let it go."

The guys had been bothering me about it for the last hour. Pro locker rooms are full of game talk, more than nonsense, but today, thanks to Zara being asleep during my touchdown, I earned the ribbing. But Micah—he always sees things through a practical lens. He's been with us two seasons. Last year, we nearly made the playoffs. This year? After today's performance, we might just go all the way.

Still, I've got work to do. I have to figure out how to beat guys like Chauncy Boyd. I managed one touchdown, but he shut me down the rest of the game. Defenses around the league are going to study tape on how he did it. Which means I'll be spending hours watching the same game film.

The locker room is nearly empty now. I took an extra-long shower—needed it to decompress.

Before I got in, one of the event staff passed a message to Liam, our locker room attendant: *Zara wants a word with you.*

Nope.

I have nothing to say to her. She messed up. Roger was right. I was wrong. He's already working to fix this mess. And honestly, I'm okay with that. If she can't respect me or show up when it counts, then we're finished.

I open my locker, reach into my jacket, and feel my phone buzzing in the pocket. Unknown number. 3-2-3 area code. L.A.

The call ends.

I check the missed call log. The same number has called five times in the last ten minutes.

I stare at the screen, trying to decide if I care enough to call back. And then it buzzes again.

I swipe to answer. "Hello?"

"Jaxon?" The voice is breathless. Nervous. Panicked."It's me… Zara."

I pause. Let the silence sit for a second. "What do you want?"

"I'm sorry," she says quickly. "But I need your help."

I close my eyes. Exhale through my nose.

I should hang up.

"Please," she whispers hoarsely. "Pretty please."

And still—I didn't hang up.

TWENTY-FOUR

The night is bitter cold—just above freezing.

I forgot a coat. Didn't bring a jacket. I nearly ducked into a department store to grab something off the rack, but I couldn't risk being recognized.

So I walk fast.

I only really feel the cold when I stop at a crosswalk or hit a red light. Otherwise, as long as I keep moving and avoid the main crowds, I stay warm enough. And unnoticed.

I'm standing in front of a closed hair salon and barbershop on 6th Avenue. I have no idea what Jaxon's car looks like, but I gave him the address and he agreed to pick me up. That was seventeen minutes ago.

I check the time on my phone again, wondering if he's actually coming—or if he said yes just to screw with me. That would be more in line with what I've come to expect from the people who drift into my life. I often ask myself how I keep attracting the same kind of assholes. Friends or lovers, it doesn't seem to matter —they're all smiles at first, all charm and sweetness, until one day—out of nowhere—they start proving I can't trust them. And once they start, they don't stop.

Still, to Jaxon's credit, he's never pretended to be nice. He's been a jerk since day one.

I shiver as I sigh, just about ready to give up and figure out another plan.

Then a huge black SUV rolls up in front of me. The passenger-side door swings open automatically. Jaxon's behind the wheel.

I rush inside like my life depends on it, shut the door, and hug myself as the heat begins to thaw my bones.

"You okay?" Jaxon asks, reaching to turn up the heat.

"My own fault. I forgot to bring a jacket," I say through chattering teeth.

He suddenly climbs out of the vehicle. Cold air rushes in as the back hatch opens. Moments later, the motorized door shuts again, and he reappears.

"Cover up," he says, handing me a long, black cashmere duster.

It smells divine—his cologne. It's the same scent I caught in the elevator that day we were headed to our first meeting with Anne and Roger. He never wore it on set. Maybe that's for the best. Because this scent? I love it.

I wrap the coat around me, resisting the urge to inhale it like a creep.

"Could you just take me to the airport?" I ask, finally sounding more like myself and less like a half-frozen puppy.

His head tilts. "When are you going to say it? You never say it."

I blink. "Say what?"

"Thank you. Say thank you."

I roll the moment back in my head. Did I not say it? "Didn't I—?"

"No," he says flatly. "You didn't."

He's handsome. Annoyingly so. Especially when he's staring at me like that. I *felt* the thanks. I even *thought* it. But... who demands gratitude?

Still. I need him.

"Thank you," I say, curtly. "Could you take me to the airport now? I would really appreciate that and have a multitude of thankfulness in my heart for it. Really, I would."

I'm being a jerk and I know it. But I can't help myself. And I honestly wouldn't be surprised if he kicked me out of the car.

Instead, he turns his eyes forward and pulls off. The SUV moves so smoothly it's like floating.

"We've got a meeting in L.A. early tomorrow. I planned to drive back tonight. I'll take you with me."

He says it like a decree. Like a king whose word is final.

Every cell in my body wants to resist. I stare at his profile, trying to figure out what to say. It's freezing outside, and this car is warm and comfortable. But it's *him* I want to get away from.

"I have to stop at my place first," he adds. "If you're hungry, I'll call ahead to room service. They can have something ready when we arrive. Unless you're still full from that sandwich."

I tense. Does he mean the po'boy I was caught scarfing down like I hadn't eaten in weeks?

"Was that supposed to be a joke, an insult, or is that just your personality?"

He snorts. "It was a joke. Sorry if it didn't land."

"You're not great at joking," I mutter. "Remember what you said about the girls and their 'girlish figures'? That wasn't funny either."

He glances over, suddenly more serious.

"You know how many women struggle with body image? Hearing the guy they're supposed to be falling for make a crack about them needing to eat less? That sticks."

He falls silent. Then: "Did I really say that?"

"You did."

"Damn." He rubs his jaw. "That wasn't what I meant. Honestly, I thought women liked that kind of stuff."

"You did?"

"They were always talking about how bloated they felt, how they'd gained weight since filming started. I told production to ease up on the alcohol—it was too much. I guess I was being sarcastic, but if it came off cruel... I'm sorry."

It's the most I've ever heard him say in a single breath. He even sounds... humbled. Like he actually cares. Which is interesting.

"Apology accepted," I whisper, feeling—for the first time—that maybe it's time I extend him some grace.

A beat passes. "So... are you hungry? We're almost there."

I glance out the window. The pier is just across the street. My guess? He lives in one of the tall buildings facing the ocean.

I shake my head. "No, I'm fine." Then I remember the earlier conversation. "But... thank you for asking."

He glances over, his brow lifting in mild surprise. Then he nods.

"You're welcome."

TWENTY-FIVE

J axon asks if I mind waiting in the SUV while he runs up to grab his things. We're parked outside his building, where a doorman stands like a sentry beneath a chandeliered lobby and floor-to-ceiling glass. He tells me he packed before the game—already planning to leave for L.A. tonight.

I'm curious, of course. I want to see what his place looks like. But just before the vehicle stopped, a call lit up the dash screen: Daphne – Pretty.

That's how he saved her in his phone. *Daphne – Pretty.* Is that his way of reminding himself she's hot? Or... what?

I found it tasteless. And yes—that's exactly why I chose to stay in the car. I wasn't about to linger while he took her call like I didn't exist.

So now I sit. Fuming. Wondering if he even

remembers he's supposed to have a *girlfriend*. Or maybe he just doesn't care.

But God, I'm tired. The longer I wait, the more my body begs for sleep. Still, I refuse. Not again. I can't risk him coming back to find me drooling in his front seat like I did during his touchdown.

Although, if he hadn't scored, none of this would've gone viral in the first place.

I scowl at myself. What a petty, selfish thought. Maybe Jaxon's right about me. Maybe there *is* a streak of selfishness I haven't faced.

Still, I wonder... *how bad did it look?*

I pull out my phone and search: Zara Morgan sleeping at football game.

I gasp.

The sheer number of clips is staggering. Apparently, I was caught sleeping *before* the touchdown. And snoring.

Oh my God—I was *snoring*.

I scroll from one video to the next.

And the next.

And the next.

"Oh shit, oh shit, oh shit," I whisper.

This isn't just bad. It's catastrophic.

"I'm in trouble."

Just then, the driver's door opens.

I nearly drop my phone, shoving it into my purse so fast I fumble the zipper.

Jaxon slides in, not saying a word. In his hands are

two large takeout cartons—burgers, fries, probably something greasy and amazing. The scent floods the car, warm and comforting and completely at odds with the panic still buzzing in my chest.

"I didn't know what you liked," he says, handing one box to me. "So I just got everything."

"Thanks," I say quietly, wishing I could crawl inside the box and disappear.

TWENTY-SIX

I plugged my address into his GPS, and now we're on the road. I can't wait to get home.

Too bad I'm not hungry, because the food smells amazing. Rich, buttery, warm. But my stomach's too knotted to touch it. Meanwhile, the burger disappears into Jaxon's hand like it's nothing more than a slider. I remind myself—he's an athlete. Food is fuel. After a game like that, he needs it.

The dashboard lights up again. No ringtone this time—he must've silenced it. But the name flashing across the screen makes my eyes widen.

Tiffany with the nice ass.

Seriously?

I shake my head, disgust crawling under my skin.

"Hey, Tiff," he answers, casual as anything, like she's an old friend. His voice is light. Warm. Flirtatious.

His right arm grips the steering wheel like a wall between us.

"She was tired. She works hard," he says. He doesn't look my way, but I can feel the judgment rolling off him. "We'll see."

The way he says *we'll see* makes my chest clench.

"Tiff, good to hear from you…"

A pause. Then laughter. A kind I've never heard from him.

"Nah… Nah… Can't do that anymore."

The sound of it—him laughing that way with her —twists something sharp in my stomach.

"Goodbye, Tiffany."

He ends the call and immediately breaks the law by picking up his phone and fiddling with it. My head's spinning. Do I call him out? Pretend I don't care? Keep quiet?

I try. Really, I do.

"I thought women hated you?" I blurt out.

His eyes stay on the road. "Not the women I know."

I scoff. "You mean women with nice asses?"

Jaxon chuckles, not at all apologetic. "Sorry you had to see that. We started one way, and now we're friends. She's married now."

I frown. "Then what can't you do with her anymore?"

"Sometimes we'd hit this private club after games.

It could get wild—too wild. I can't be seen there for a while. At least not for six months." He winks.

"Oh," I say. That makes sense. Sort of.

He glances at me. "What about you?"

"What about me?"

"A few of the ladies said you told them you'd introduce them to better guys than me."

My eyes roll almost involuntarily. Of course those words would come back to haunt me now.

"I know some decent guys," I say with a shrug. "Didn't mean I was dating any of them."

"Who were you dating?"

I pause. Toby Lane flashes to mind. Real name: Blaine Bello from Dayton, Ohio. He was a walking red flag who couldn't keep it in his pants.

"Wasn't it Toby Lane?" Jaxon asks, cutting into my silence.

My head snaps toward him. "How do you know that?"

"I looked it up."

"You researched me?"

"I would hope you researched me."

I go silent. Because, no—I didn't. Not really. I barely thought about Jaxon until yesterday. And now, sitting next to him in this warm car, I realize Roger had been right. I hadn't taken any of this seriously. Not the gig. Not Jaxon. Not what it would mean if we failed.

He lets out a low snort. That tells me he's having the same thoughts as I am.

There's so much I could say. About Toby. About all the guys before him. About how I always seem to fall for the ones who hurt me and ignore the ones who never would. How the women from the show feel exactly the same—they love me until it stops serving them, and then they're out.

But I don't say any of that.

Because I don't trust Jaxon with it.

Instead, I close my eyes and pretend to sleep. It's safer that way. Safer than blurting something I'll regret. Easier than admitting that I can feel it—he's done. Done pretending. Done playing boyfriend. Done with *me*.

TWENTY-SEVEN

"Zara."

Jaxon's voice cuts through the fog in my head, snapping me awake. My eyes flutter open, and I jolt upright, disoriented for a second—until I remember where I am.

I glance out the window.

We're parked in front of my house, the SUV idling before the closed gate. I turn to Jaxon, who's watching me with a mixture of curiosity and amusement.

"I slept the whole way?" I ask, my voice rough with sleep.

He nods. "Pretty much."

"Wow." I reach into my purse, digging for my keys. I press the button on my fob, and the iron gates begin to glide open, retreating into the thick privacy hedges lining my driveway.

As we drive up the cobblestone turnabout toward the front door, my house looks... cozy. Safe. Welcoming in a way I didn't expect after a night like this.

"Nice place," Jaxon says, his voice low as he surveys the exterior.

"Thanks." I unclip my seatbelt as the SUV rolls to a gentle stop. I hesitate for a moment, then turn to him. "Do you want to come in? Just for a drink... or if you need the bathroom?"

It's a courtesy. Polite. Not meant to be taken literally.

But he surprises me.

"Sure," he says.

IT'S A LITTLE ODD HAVING JAXON HERE. HE'S SO TALL and broad-shouldered that he almost seems too large for my cozy hallways and modest-sized rooms.

I hand him a bottle of water before showing him around.

"It's really well decorated," he says once we're in the living room. "I like the color palette—browns, tans, whites. Clean. Warm."

"Thanks," I say. "Me too."

We smile at each other—polite and distant, like the kind of friends we certainly aren't.

"Come on," I say. "I'll show you the backyard."

And truthfully, I don't mind showing him. There's something nice about sharing this part of my life, my space, with someone—even if it's him.

Out back, I point to the casita.

"I use that mostly for yoga and Pilates. And over there," I gesture toward a small, slightly raised area with lighting, "is my practice stage. I run lines there sometimes."

He grunts in interest. "Zara," he says, my name slipping out as if unprompted.

"Jaxon," I say, matching his tone.

"Oh—by the way," I add casually, "feel free to stay in the guest room tonight. It's no trouble."

We lock eyes for a beat. My heart pounds—not because I want him, but because I can see it in his face. That sullen, heavy look. He's about to say something I don't want to hear.

"I have a place in Century City," he replies.

"You do?" I say, surprised.

"Yeah." He hesitates. "But I wanted to tell you…"

I cut him off before he can finish. "Wait—before you do, I just want to say I'm sorry for falling asleep today. I get it. I really do. I'll do better. I promise."

But his mouth tightens at the corners, his expression growing heavy again.

That's when I know.

He rubs the inside corners of his eyes. "Roger's done with the arrangement," he says. "And… we're going with Ashley. Just thought I should give you a heads-up."

I go still.

And yet, I feel nothing.

Not shock. Not hurt. Just… a strange, hollow numbness.

It's the same feeling I had when I showed up at Blaine's house—groceries in hand, planning to surprise him with a birthday dinner—only to find him in bed with not one, but two women. I didn't cry. Didn't scream. Just dropped the groceries and walked away.

I'd seen the signs with Blaine. Chose to ignore them. And there it was, in my face.

Just like now.

I nod, calmly. "It's fair," I say.

After a moment, he echoes it. "Yeah."

I take a deep breath—steady, resigned. I still feel nothing. Not yet. But deep down, I know I'm to blame. I fumbled something important, and now the cost is coming due.

"Well," I say, "see you tomorrow."

"See you tomorrow," he replies.

I walk him to the front, point him down the path that curves around to the driveway. I listen for the soft start of the SUV engine, the quiet crunch of tires on cobblestone. The gate closes automatically behind him.

And that's when I feel it.

Not devastation. Not betrayal.

Just the sharp, cold certainty of square one.

Back at the beginning.

Still in trouble.

My shot at redemption?

Blown to hell.

And I have no one to blame but myself.

TWENTY-EIGHT

THE NEXT DAY

The funny thing is, I slept well last night.

Despite the weight of everything Jaxon said—despite knowing my world had likely blown apart—I went to bed, closed my eyes, and drifted into the kind of sleep that only comes after total resignation.

I don't even know if I'll still have *Next In Line* after today, but strangely... I'm okay with that. It feels almost inevitable, like this is how things were always going to turn out.

I arrive early to Anne's office. She asked for a premeeting before our official meeting with the network. I never told her what Jaxon said last night—about Roger pulling the plug. I half expected her to call and chew me out already, but she didn't. That silence makes me think things are worse than I imagined.

Maybe she's going to drop me as a client today too.

If so, by the end of this meeting, I'll have neither a new gig nor an agent. Just a reputation that's one viral nap away from washed up. But I'll figure it out. I haven't blown through my money—I knew better than that. I've saved well, and I bought my house outright. I can coast for a while.

Still, I feel... nothing.

I park in my usual spot near the elevators. The building's air conditioning is overactive as always, but it barely registers. I ride up to Anne's floor and nod to the receptionist, who seems far too bubbly.

Does she know?

Anne's assistant appears, beaming. "Would you like coffee, water, tea?"

"No thanks," I say with a slight shake of my head. My stomach is the only part of me still capable of feeling—and right now, it wants nothing inside it.

"Well, let me know if you need anything," she offers as she opens Anne's door.

We both know I won't. It's just something people say, another part of the Hollywood script. Maybe that's why everything's unraveling for me—I'm tired of reading lines I didn't write. I want off this soundstage.

Anne has a finger raised, mid-call, signaling me to

wait. I sit quietly on the couch, where I always sit during these meetings. Across from her desk. Below her perch.

"Right… right," she says into the phone. "I thought so. Just wanted to make sure."

She hangs up and then, with a voice too bright for the news I know is coming, says, "How are we doing this morning?"

"Fine," I murmur.

"Let's get to it. Roger wants to pull the deal."

I close my eyes, exhaling hard. "I know. They have every right. I saw all the videos. I was snoring. My mouth was open. It was terrible. I learned the entire episode one script. I'm ready. But…"

"Zara," Anne says, cutting me off. "Be quiet."

I go still.

She rises from behind her desk and walks over to sit beside me on the sofa. That alone stuns me. I've heard her say, more than once, that a power player never sits eye-level with a client. Always keep the height difference, even if it's an inch.

So when she sits next to me now, something is different.

"You were overstretched yesterday," she says gently. "You didn't mean to fall asleep. You don't understand football—and honestly, I think that shit is boring too. But more importantly, I have to take some accountability here. I should've insisted you get an assistant years ago. You said you had it all under control, and back then, you did. But things are different now. You're reaching new heights."

She pauses, holding my gaze. "And *Next In Line*? I'm not letting that go."

Before I can speak, her phone buzzes. She hops up, answering immediately.

"They're here?" Her eyebrows lift. Whatever she hears pleases her. "Don't offer coffee or tea or anything. Just bring them straight in."

Anne carefully places the phone back in its cradle, then locks eyes with me.

"Are you ready to stop fucking around and be the professional I know you are?"

I nod without hesitation. "Very much so."

She gives me a sly wink. "Good."

TWENTY-NINE

JAXON WILDE

I'm still on the fence about the plan. Zara's a risk. Falling asleep during the game was a huge miss. You don't need a PR expert to tell you that someone who passes out during your touchdown doesn't love you—or even like you, really. Which is fine. But if you're pretending to be someone's girlfriend, the bare minimum is staying awake.

I can't risk that again. I've lived through the high-pitched boos every time I touched the ball. The kind of backlash that sticks. People labeled me a misogynistic prick, and that shit echoed louder than any cheer. Things are better now. The show stitched together a different side of me. I'm still not Prince Charming, but I'm not their villain anymore either. I'm just… a guy.

We stop just short of Anne's assistant. Roger leans in close.

"This is it," he says under his breath. "I'll drop the hammer. Then we copter back to San Diego and start building your new storyline with Ashley. She's in." He winks like it's a done deal. He's proud of himself—relieved, honestly. Ending things with Anne is a win for him. He doesn't like her.

He's ranted more than once about how she "threw her dick" in his face the day she stood while he sat during a pitch. I wasn't there, but I've heard it enough. Roger doesn't respect strong women. He sees force where there's just confidence.

But I see Anne differently. She's tough. Strategic. She gets shit done.

Roger? He's the real misogynist in the room.

Still—I shrug. Like I said, I'm on the fence.

"I can't copter back. I drove up last night," I say, leaving out *with Zara*. He'd hit the roof if I told him.

"Then I'll have Lloyd from the L.A. office drive your car back. You need to be in San Diego with me to kick off this new campaign."

I don't like this plan, but I don't want to oppose it right now. I'll wait until after the meeting.

Anne's assistant perks up the second she spots us and walks us to the office. Inside, Anne is leaning against her massive desk, calm and composed. Zara's already seated on the couch.

I let out a low, involuntary laugh. Now I see it.

That couch is a tactic. Last time I sat on it, I thought it was just low. But no—it's by design. Like the armchair Roger avoids. They drop your eye level so Anne's always physically looking down on you. It's brilliant.

"Gentlemen," Anne says, gesturing to the seats.

"I'll stand," Roger snaps, already irritated. He's caught on to her power play.

"This won't take long," he says.

"We've been talking, and—" Anne starts at the same time.

She pauses, holding out a hand to give him the floor.

If I were Roger, I'd decline. I can see it in Anne's eyes—she's not desperate. She's holding something.

"We tried to make a deal," Roger begins, "but for the good of the organization, we've decided to take this campaign in a new direction."

"You can't," Anne replies smoothly. "Your organization is under contract with mine. And before we go any further, Zara has something she'd like to say."

Roger waves his hands like he's clearing the air of something foul. "No way. I got authorization."

Anne crosses her arms, completely unfazed. "From who?"

The pinch of skin between Roger's eyebrows tightens. His lips press together. He doesn't answer.

Anne pushes up from her desk—calm, controlled. She lifts her phone.

"Get George Baldwin on the line," she tells her assistant.

Roger breaks. "Okay. We'll do it your way—for now."

Anne sets the phone down, unbothered. "Never mind." She turns to Zara. "Your turn."

Zara looks straight at me. No walls. No spin. Just clear, raw sincerity. And in that moment, she's stunning. Pretty, yes—but not just that. Vulnerable. Real. The kind of woman I'd want to shield from vultures like Roger.

"I'm so, so sorry," she says. "I'll bring my full attention and professionalism to this project. And I'll try to love football too."

Anne glances at Roger. "That good enough for you?"

His stare could cut steel. "For now—yes."

Anne snorts a soft, mocking chuckle—the kind a fighter throws across the ring before landing a punch.

"Excellent," she says, voice bright as a lollipop. "And I have a plan so ironclad, there'll be no more hiccups. People are going to believe these two are having more sex than rabbits."

She turns to Zara.

"Pack your things. You're moving to San Diego. Tonight."

"What?" Zara stumbles to her feet. "I can't move to San Diego. I start shooting in—"

"Production is delayed. You start filming in three months. That gives us time to wrangle this in," Anne says. "You can come home when Jaxon's on the road, but when he's in San Diego, your pretty ass better be there with him."

She snatches a sheet of paper from her desk and straight-arms it toward Zara. "Meet Kat Lake, your assistant. She starts today. She'll call you three times a day with your schedule. When you need something—anything—you call her. She'll have an office at the agency and at your home, so make space."

Zara blinks, stunned. "Huh?"

Anne fixes her with a cold stare. "Don't fuck this up again."

THIRTY

Yet again, Jaxon and I find ourselves riding down in the elevator together. He seems just as wonderstruck as I am. It's not like him to let silence reign for too long, but yes—he's been bewildered into silence.

"That was... interesting," I say, needing to take his temperature.

"Agreed."

"But this... living with you. She can't *seriously* mean—"

My chiming phone steals my attention. It's a message from my new assistant, Kat Lake.

Kat Lake, Monday 10:32 AM

A car will be at your house at 1:30 PM to drive you to Jaxon Wilde's apartment. Please be packed. I will be at your place before then to pick up a key and a gate opener. If you don't have a spare, I'll take care of it. Thank you for this opportunity. It will be a pleasure to meet you.—KL

"Look." I hold up my phone to show Jaxon the message. "This is really happening. It's a nightmare."

Gradually—like watching the sun drop behind a mountain—Jaxon's open, curious expression twists into irritation.

"This is your fault. Not mine."

I grunt. "I *know* this. I screwed up. I get it. Jeez. Do you always have to be an asshole? And please don't make this harder than it already is."

Like a snake striking, Jaxon's long arm shoots out to press the stop button.

"You know what?" he says, turning to face me. He inches closer.

And closer.

Until he's so near I can feel the heat radiating off his body. My head spins. I press myself against the wall, trying to stay upright as my heart becomes a firing range of panic and... something else.

His face inches toward mine.

I watch his tongue sweep slowly across his bottom

lip, like he's not even aware of doing it. His warm, minty breath grazes my mouth. The air between us practically shimmers with tension.

We stay like this for a few seconds—but it feels like forever.

I don't know what I want from him.

Push him away?

No. I don't want that.

Kiss him?

God, no. I shouldn't want that.

The space between my thighs throbs. Reaches. Do I want *that*?

No.

No way.

Then slowly—his sexy mouth moves closer to my left ear.

"I won't be home when you arrive," he murmurs. "I have recovery today. But look around. Make yourself comfortable."

A pause.

"And be nice to me, Zara. I've earned it. Don't you think?"

Oh shit.

His nearness is driving me insane. And I know this isn't about him personally—I don't *like* Jaxon. I hate him. It's just that... it's been too long. He's a walking aphrodisiac. When this is over, I need to start dating again. For real.

"Is that a yes?" he asks, lips still at my ear.

He's not going to move until I say something. I can feel it.

"Um-hmm," I manage.

"Good."

Finally, I'm released from the prison of his nearness.

I stare at his back as he presses the start button. The doors slide open immediately.

And I'm still speechless as Jaxon strolls out of the elevator like he doesn't just own the world—

He owns me too.

THIRTY-ONE

SIX HOURS LATER

What a day. I met Kat, who's smart, efficient, and fully capable. It's been less than a full day since she came into my life, and already she's making things easier. That alone terrifies me. I don't want to get used to it. I don't want to run her off. Or worse—what if she leaves on her own?

Assistants in this industry rarely stay in one place for long. And then there's me. Everyone who enters my life eventually leaves it—gone for good. That's true for my family—well, my father's side, which is the only family I have left. It's true for every friend I've picked up along the way. Nobody stuck around after my shoplifting incident. The only friend I have left is

Anne. And sometimes, I wonder if I weren't her client, would she have ghosted me too?

My mind has been spinning with these kinds of thoughts ever since I got into the back of this black hired car with tinted windows, its trunk packed with all my essentials. I brought my laptop and my extra-large monitor. My tea kettle. My warm socks. My baggy sweats—one for every day of the week.

According to my new schedule, Jaxon's next game is Thursday night. Since he's on the road traveling to an away game on Saturday, I'll be able to go back home that morning. I can hardly wait.

I also plan to be *prepared* for game night in more ways than one. I'll wear something vaguely in the WAG category—without fully crossing into WAGville. I can look stylish without trying to give Jaxon a hard-on all the way up in our private little section. I packed enough outfits to test a few and see what works. No heels, though. I'm not wearing high heels to a football game. That's where I draw the line.

"Miss?"

The driver's voice pulls me out of my anxious thoughts.

"Yes?" I answer, startled, my voice jumpy.

"I said, you don't have to worry about your things. Kat arranged for valet service to bring everything up."

Valet? "Is this a hotel?"

"Not to my knowledge," he says, amused. "I was told it's a full-service condominium."

"Oh," I murmur. Then I remember Jaxon's voice telling me to *be nice*. "Thank you."

I wish I could stay in the car forever. I imagine his apartment is a typical bachelor setup—leather couches, neon beer signs, maybe even a pool table smack in the middle of the living room. But whatever it is, I'm bracing for a mess. Still, I muster the courage —and the will—and push the door open.

"Here goes... everything," I whisper as I step out, now standing on the curb.

My pulse races. My stomach flips.

God, I wish this didn't have to happen.

THIRTY-TWO

The process goes smoother than I expected.

Anita handles it—a woman who looks to be in her mid-twenties, all long, glossy black hair that she flips every so often like punctuation. Her red dress is tight, her heels high and loud. She's the one assigned to program my fingerprint into the system so I can access every elevator in the building—especially the ones leading to Jaxon's private residence and the garage, where a parking space awaits me, should I ever decide to drive my own car.

"You also have free access to our rental car service through Jaxon," she says after asking me to test the elevator by pressing my fingertip to the glass pad.

A green light flashes. The doors slide open. Everything works.

"Perfect," she says, satisfied.

She steps in beside me. Once the doors close and the elevator begins its silent climb, I catch the full force of her perfume. It's nothing like what the WAGs wear—sweet, sophisticated, the scent of restraint. Hers is heavy, almost edible, wrapping the small space until I can taste it. The air thickens. My stomach turns.

"Jaxon is one of our premier residents. He's so personal and down-to-earth. All the girls love him. You know…" She shrugs a shoulder. "He's the best."

I smile. This is the part where I'm supposed to say something to prove I agree—that he's so damn great, the best boyfriend in the world, and how lucky I am to have found him. Something like that.

But all she does is trigger a memory I've worked hard to suppress—successfully, until now. Jaxon, too close, his lips near mine, my desire battling my will. This little thing between us isn't real. It's fake and will always stay that way.

Thankfully, she doesn't require a response. The doors slide open, revealing a sun-drenched entryway that feels more like an art gallery than a hallway. We step onto polished concrete floors, reflecting the natural light pouring in through floor-to-ceiling windows just beyond.

"Wow," is all I can manage as I take in the shimmering blue of the Pacific, the curve of the marina, and the clusters of anchored boats bobbing gently in the harbor.

"I know. It's quite stunning, especially for one gorgeous, single man." The way her eyes flit across my face—she's looking for a reaction.

I fold my arms across my chest, letting an old, uncomfortable sensation ripple through my stomach. The last time I felt this way was when Blaine broke my heart—known publicly as ladies' man Toby Lane.

I don't want to feel this way, especially not while Anita continues her tour, showing off a stylish living room with low-profile Italian sectionals anchoring the wide-open space. A glass coffee table disappears almost entirely into the design. I never thought of Jaxon as an art person, but among the succulents in concrete planters are a few well-chosen abstract murals that add tasteful pops of color.

One side of the room features an enormous television mounted to the wall.

"He likes hanging out in this room," she says, eyes again drifting to gauge my reaction.

The more she drops these little hints about knowing Jaxon personally, the easier it is to forget our elevator moment earlier. That? That was a game. He was trying to seduce me into submission.

Well, it didn't work.

Cue slightly jealous girlfriend.

"And you know this how?" I ask, injecting the perfect amount of agitation.

"Oh…" She chuckles happily, oddly satisfied. "Sometimes he calls for help, and I come by and he's here, watching TV. Or I help out with room service, you know."

I can't help but grin at how obvious she's being—which isn't exactly on script. I should be a little infuriated, not amused by how hard she's trying to stake her claim on my fake boyfriend.

"Oh, and speaking of room service," she continues, leading me into the kitchen, "you have 24-hour access for all meals. You seriously never have to cook. Concierge handles laundry and dry cleaning. There's daily maid service."

Why would Jaxon have a kitchen like this if he never intended to cook in it? It's a proper chef's kitchen, outfitted with high-end stainless steel appliances and a full barista setup. I probably won't need my plug-in tea kettle after all. The floating curved island, lit from below with a soft ambient glow, adds to the illusion of weightlessness. Its edges are wrapped in sleek wood paneling, and the top is a slab of pristine white marble.

She keeps going—shows me a state-of-the-art workout room, a theater where she claims Jaxon reviews game footage (again, how does she know?), a sauna, jacuzzi, and even a massage table.

"Let me guess—you sometimes massage him?" I ask, smirking.

"I'm a trained masseuse," she announces proudly.

I burst out laughing. "No way."

Her eyes widen, clearly unsure what's funny.

I shake my head as my laughter fades. "So, um, does he get happy endings?"

Her jaw drops. "Excuse me?" Her face pinches into something between offense and scandal.

I tilt my head, surprised by her reaction. I know her type. They love to toe the line and then act offended when someone calls them on it.

"You've been hinting at how well you know my boyfriend since we started this little tour, and now you tell me you're his masseuse…"

"I didn't say that," she snaps, defensive. "Don't tell him I said that—you'd be lying."

I narrow my eyes. Frankly, I'm over this tour. I'm tired and ready to be alone.

"Okay, whatever. Where's my bedroom? Did Jaxon tell you where it is?"

Without a word, she stomps off like a petulant child. I follow her down a long hallway lined with private rooms until she stops at one that feels like a five-star coastal retreat.

The moment I step inside, I feel calm. Muted tones of sand, cream, and driftwood gray create a sense of quiet luxury. A king-sized bed dressed in crisp white linens and layered with a peach cashmere throw sits beneath a large abstract canvas in soft ocean hues. Walnut nightstands hold sculptural lamps that cast a warm, ambient glow. Floor-to-ceiling windows offer a partial view of the marina.

"You have blackout shades all around," Anita

says, clearly annoyed now. She demonstrates how they work.

Her tone shifts toward professional again as she shows me how to open the media cabinet and use another massive television.

Then we enter the spa bathroom. She demonstrates the heated marble floors. I take in the free-standing soaking tub under a skylight, a walk-in rain shower with floor-to-ceiling stone tile, a teak bench, eucalyptus bundles hanging from the brass rainfall head, a floating double vanity framed in pale oak, soft-close drawers, creamy quartz counters, backlit mirrors, and heated towel racks.

I didn't expect this level of luxury. I might need to step up my home game. Still, I'm genuinely impressed with Jaxon's taste.

"What's that?" I ask, pointing back in the bedroom.

A card and a bundle of silver-foil chocolates rest on one of the pillows.

"Looks like a note," she says.

I pick it up. It's from Jaxon.

Remember, Sweet.

JM

I snort and roll my eyes.

"We're done. Goodbye," Anita says, turning on her heels and leaving abruptly.

It's only when I start to drop my jaw in response to her dramatic exit that I realize I'm smiling. I don't think she liked how much Jaxon's little note made me grin. And there was nothing to be jealous of. Had she stuck around a moment longer, I might've even read it to her. Not that she would've understood.

Oh well.

I pop a chocolate in my mouth and head to order lunch.

Oddly, and thankfully, my appetite's back—and I'm starving.

THIRTY-THREE

Nearly an hour later, I've unpacked my clothes, put away the bare essentials, and decided to leave my tea kettle tucked safely in my luggage. Once everything found its rightful place, the concierge sent an attendant to collect my suitcases and garment bags for storage—even though there's more than enough space in the gigantic walk-in closet, which is honestly a room unto itself. Still, I let them take the bags. If they stay in sight, Jaxon might drive me so crazy I'll be tempted to pack up and make a run for it.

But the truth is, this is overwhelming.

Never in a million years did I imagine living with this kind of convenience. As a B+ actress—just the right project away from tipping into the A-list—I *could* afford a lifestyle like this... if I were willing to waste money. But since it's not *my* money I'd be wasting, I give myself permission to indulge in the perks. I order a chicken club sandwich with a garden-fresh salad. I'm starving.

Still, before my food arrives, I check out the kitchen. It's the one room I know I'll need to learn inside and out.

I open the massive stainless steel Sub-Zero fridge and gasp—it's spotless, fully stocked, and meticulously organized. Items are arranged by type and stored in labeled glass containers. Each one has its nutritional info printed on top. Wow. Jaxon might actually be a little anal-retentive.

Next, I investigate the barista setup. It's a beauty. Once upon a time, when I first moved to L.A., I worked at one of those coffee shops where every other barista is hoping to get discovered. I was good at it. Actually, I loved that job. So naturally, I get to work.

I brew a fresh shot of espresso, steam the milk, find a porcelain cup in the cabinet, and make myself the cutest little cappuccino—complete with a perfect foam heart on top.

"Mmm," I hum, rolling my eyes back with delight.

The girl's still got it.

I take a deep breath and try to reset, grounding myself in this foreign yet oddly welcoming space. I still can't believe I'm here. But maybe, if I stay focused on work and ignore everything else, I can survive being in Jaxon's personal world. For now, I'll tolerate being outside my comfort zone—because Thursday's game is coming fast, and I've got a lot to do before then.

I finish my cappuccino in a few quick sips, grab a bottle of artisanal water from the fridge, and then—ding-dong.

The doorbell rings.

"Room service!" a voice calls out through a speaker system.

Wow. Again… the perks.

TODAY'S TASK? LEARN FOOTBALL.

After devouring lunch, I set myself up in the living room—because the screen is so massive it practically watches me back. I find the remote magnetically docked to the side of the screen and hit the *Power* button.

The TV chimes to life. Smart, of course. Thankfully, Jaxon subscribes to a million sports channels. I pick one dedicated to football.

Soon, I'm watching men in uniforms huddled together—or wait, maybe that's not a huddle. They're more like... lined up? One side facing the other like dueling soldiers. And then—bam. They crash each other like human car accidents. The collision is so loud I wince.

"Damn," I mutter.

From the stands, it didn't seem so brutal. But up close, like this? I'm shocked this is legal.

I lean back against the couch, torn between fascination and secondhand pain. The action halts. The screen says *2nd & 8*, whatever that means.

The commentators are no help—talking fast and furious, tossing around terms like "blitz," "snap count," and "nickel defense" as if everyone already has a PhD in football.

More clashing. More shouting. Someone throws the ball, another guy catches it—and...

"Yikes!" I yelp.

The poor guy gets *slammed* to the ground. That was aggressive. Vicious even.

I've heard of flag football. Can't they just pull a ribbon off someone's waist and call it a day? Why does it have to be... *this*?

No wonder Jaxon's body is built like a granite sculpture. He has to endure this kind of violence regularly.

Another lineup. A whistle blows. Everyone resets.

I sigh, frustrated. *Why are they stopping now?*

Something about "offside" is mentioned. But no one explains what it means in a way I understand. The ambient noise, the shouts, the commentators chattering—it's all beginning to blur. Add in the comforting hum of the TV, the plush couch, and my post-lunch food coma, and...

I feel it coming.

The cappuccino I made earlier was supposed to keep me alert. Clearly, it failed. I tell myself I'll just close my eyes for one minute. Just one.

I will open them again.

I will.

But just like Sunday night at the stadium, sleep creeps up on me—and wins.

THIRTY-FOUR

JAXON WILDE

The TV is blaring when I step into my apartment. I'd been wondering what Zara had been doing all day. Watching football wasn't anywhere on my list of guesses.

I walk into the living room and stop cold.

She's on the couch, head back, chin up, *snoring*. The Jacksonville versus Cincinnati game from yesterday is playing on the screen.

Is she a Bengals fan? Jaguars?

I spot the remote beside her on the cushion and press mute.

"Zara?" I say softly.

Not yet. I don't really want to wake her. Not right now.

What the hell was that earlier? Why did I push her like that in the elevator?

Did I want her?

Yeah. I did.

But I have to keep that shit under control. She's not safe. She's selfish as hell. Always infuriating. An actress, playing a role—but sometimes, damn it, she gets to me.

Like in Anne's office. That apology was real. I could tell.

But in the elevator? When she said, *"It's a nightmare"*? That stung. Is that how she sees me?

I glance back at the screen and it hits me—football put her to sleep again.

She doesn't like the game. Still, she'd better not fall asleep in the arena again. We can't afford that kind of attention.

"Zara," I say louder this time.

Nothing.

I reach down and gently shake her knee. "Zara!"

She bolts upright, wide-eyed and panicked. "What? Did I fall asleep?" She locks onto me. "Jaxon? What time is it?"

I check my watch. "Seven thirty-three."

"Nooo," she groans, slumping forward. "I slept through the game. *Again?*" Her mouth turns down and she looks up at me with these helpless, glassy eyes.

Damn.

I want to kiss her. We've never kissed, but I want to. Just once.

Just *once*.

I swallow hard—fighting the ache in my chest, the throb in my tricot track pants.

No.

No way.

No.

Way.

"What's the problem, Zara? The game bores you?"

She shrugs. "I don't know. I just don't understand it. Why do they stop so often? Why do they keep slamming into each other? And what do all the numbers mean? It's just... confusing. That's all. And I've never been into sports."

I cross my arms and nod. I can see what she needs now.

"So you need to learn the game?"

She shifts upright, suddenly alert. "I guess so."

"Want me to teach you?"

Her brows shoot up like I just offered her a prison sentence. I stay still. Part of me wants to take it back —her hesitation feels like rejection.

But she needs help. And helping her helps *both* of us.

She exhales slowly. "Yes. Please. Teach me."

THIRTY-FIVE

The way he's looking at me, I almost expect him to take back the offer. But then he starts nodding.

"Follow me," he says and walks off.

I spring to my feet and trail behind him—this towering hunk of a man.

No. No, no.

I shake my head. I can't think of Jaxon that way. He's my *teacher*. Like a coach. That's better.

He leads me into his home theater and gestures for me to sit in one of the oversized black leather recliners near the front. I sink into the chair, and he takes the one next to me. He lifts a panel in the armrest to reveal a built-in control screen.

"From here, you can run everything," he says, like he's inviting me to use the space whenever I want.

As he talks me through it, I glance at his face.

Jaxon really is generous. I can't deny that. He's magnetic—until he flips the switch and becomes a complete ass. But now... I'm not so sure anymore.

He honestly thinks *I'm* the selfish one. And rude.

Maybe sometimes I am. I tend to skip small formalities. It's not that I don't feel them—I just wasn't raised to validate every moment with a "thank you" or a "you're welcome." I didn't even notice that about myself until Jaxon kept pointing it out—during the show and after.

Still, he could be a little nicer about it. At least, that's what *I* think.

"Got it," he says gruffly, finishing his tutorial.

"Got it," I echo, determined not to take his tone personally.

"Good." He flashes a smile, like I, his newly minted student, just earned my first A.

I smile back. And suddenly, we're caught in this moment—just... smiling at each other.

And here's what I know, with certainty:

If we were a real couple, I would kiss him right now.

Right after he finishes licking his bottom lip like that...

He clears his throat and finally breaks eye contact. "Buckle up," he says. "I'm taking you back through the game you slept through on Sunday night."

THIRTY-SIX

Oh my God, I can hardly keep up—but seeing Jaxon up close and on the field makes staying awake so much easier. He's like poetry in motion.

How did I not see that on Sunday night?

He explains every stoppage of play, meticulously breaking down false starts, simulated snaps meant to trick the offense into flinching, and exaggerated movements designed to bait a reaction.

I learn what the numbers mean—1st and 10, 2nd and 8, and so on. If they gain ten yards, they start over at first down again. That's a good thing. Yay!

Jaxon keeps running the ball further than ten yards anyway. He's really good. No wonder he's so popular. A lot of people in the stands are wearing his jersey.

He shows me a holding call.

"Chauncy knows how to sneak 'em in without getting caught."

He spends a lot of time walking me through Chauncy Boyd's infraction. I can tell he's irritated by Chauncy—but he respects him, too. He's clearly itching for the chance to beat him, as he put it, "man-on-man."

Time melts away as he explains a field goal and what distances are considered favorable. And how the defense kicks off when it's the offense's turn to take their 1st and 10 down the field.

So, in plain terms—Genesis actually did give me the gist of the game. All the offense has to do is make it to the opposite end of the field and score.

Jaxon goes quiet when he misses—what he calls—a perfectly thrown ball. His eyes flick up to the Jumbotron.

For the first time, the announcers say, *"He could have some distractions in the stands today."*

And then there I am, caught on camera mid-bite, gobbling a shrimp po' boy.

"Sorry," I say. "I had no idea all this was going on during a game."

"You're forgiven," he says, and winks at me.

I'm cheesing—and I wish I could stop, because he's watching my face like it's a movie screen.

"How's your lesson so far?" he finally asks.

I think he's proud of himself for keeping me interested in his game—his job, really.

"It's going great. You're a fantastic teacher."

He finally rips his eyes away from my face and gets the game moving again.

"Good. Let's get to the end."

THERE ARE SO MANY PENALTIES. EVEN JAXON RACKS up four of them. I don't like that.

I finally see why Genesis booed so loudly earlier when Barber got called for a face mask penalty. Honestly, I didn't even see him touch the other guy's face mask. And if he did, it was barely a tap.

"Sometimes the refs can be overzealous," Jaxon says.

When he's about to score, I'm perched on the edge of my seat. My heart's thudding in my chest. He's so graceful—like a jaguar or a cheetah, ball tucked between his arms and hand over it to protect it, just like he explained.

Chauncy is only a few steps behind, gaining ground. But just before the end zone, Jaxon thrusts his body forward and scores!

I leap out of my seat, cheering and celebrating—until I see what's happening on the screen. The camera has captured another version of me.

My most embarrassing moment. Ever.

Horrified, I immediately fall silent.

"Again, sorry," I mumble.

But Jaxon is beaming. He points at the TV. "Don't worry. What you just did makes up for that."

Now I'm flustered. Sitting beside him, I'm hot and bothered—and dangerously close to suggesting we do something very stupid.

And dangerous.

I mean, we're both adults.

Although… I'm not even sure Jaxon wants me, sexually. He doesn't even like me much.

"A girl named Anita gave me a tour earlier," I say, testing the waters. He might be into Anita.

"Oh yeah. Good," he says, shifting in his chair. "She's good."

There it is. That little tell. Something's going on between them. He's probably going to sneak around with her while I'm away—or worse, while I'm asleep.

And just like that, I pull myself together.

We make it to the end of the game. San Diego barely wins. We both stand.

I hold out my hand. "Thank you for this. I'm actually excited about Thursday's game now. You're going to kick their asses."

I'm surprised when he pulls me in.

This time, his hard body presses fully against mine —and yes, he's hard in all the right places.

So… he does want me.

He lowers his mouth to my left ear, and a warm, tingling sensation washes over me as I close my eyes.

"I agree," he whispers, ASMR-style.

My knees weaken as Jaxon slowly backs away—leaving me aching for more, but not totally willing to *do* more.

And I think he feels the same way. I can feel the invisible barrier he just erected between us.

"Today's been a long day," he says, thumbing over his shoulder.

I nod. "Right. Good night."

He nods back and—without another word—whips around and walks off.

I hold my breath as I watch him disappear down the hallway. When I'm sure he's far enough away, I finally exhale and collapse back into my chair.

Goodness. Is *this* how it's going to be living with Jaxon Wilde?

I've got to get a grip.

I can't let lust drown my judgment.

I have to remember—this is all an act. Jaxon and I are like night and day. Good and evil. Never and never.

THIRTY-SEVEN

The truth is, I didn't know what to do with that little interaction between Jaxon and me last night.

But when I finally made it back to my room, I took one of the best showers of my life. The steam—infused with eucalyptus—cleared my sinuses *and* my head. There was no tossing, no turning. No staring at the ceiling, wondering why my chest felt tight. None of that last night.

By the time my face hit the pillow, I felt light. Rinsed clean. Sleep came instantly.

Nope.

Anxiety just waited until morning to pounce.

It's barely past seven, and already I feel like my day is sprinting ahead without me. I practically leap out of bed, survival mode fully activated.

First: check my calendar.

Just as I remembered: a virtual table reading at nine. I exhale maybe twenty percent of my anxiety. There's time.

Second: get dressed.

I pull on a plain black cashmere sweatsuit, already thinking about my script, laptop, and extra monitor. I'm pretty sure Anita was supposed to show me my office, but after I called her out on her passive-aggressiveness, she cut the tour short.

Sliding into a pair of multicolored striped socks, I grab my phone and head out, determined to find the workspace myself.

I wonder where Jaxon's bedroom is. The last thing I need is to stumble into it by accident. I remember that all the fun stuff—the spa, gym, theater, private pool—is on the opposite side of the house. Kitchen and living room are dead center.

If my office were near any of that, Anita would've shown me.

Which means... it's probably on *this* side.

I pass a sleek powder room—minimal and elegant, like the rest of the place. Then, at the next doorway, I startle so hard my hand flies to my chest.

Shirtless, Jaxon sits cross-legged on the floor, facing the eastern city view, sunlight spilling over him like some ancient warrior-god.

His back is pure perfection. Of course.

You can't do what Jaxon does for a living and *not* be in optimal shape.

"Sorry," I blurt, just as he turns—before I can escape.

At least he doesn't look annoyed.

He pivots fully toward me.

"It's fine. How'd you sleep?"

Wow.

His *chest* is a work of art.

"Good." The word comes out too fast. Too bright.

His calm only amplifies my jitteriness.

"I'm looking for the office so I can start work. Anita didn't show me."

God, I actually feel a little upset about that.

He studies me. And the longer he does, the more intense the tingling in my chest.

"What?" I snap, suddenly defensive. "Say what you're thinking already."

He doesn't blink. "Is this how you're going to work?"

I frown, glancing down at my outfit, tugging at my ponytail—defensive and embarrassed. "What do you mean?"

He laughs softly. "Not your appearance. You look…"

He pauses, the corner of his mouth lifting.

"I mean your energy."

I straighten like a soldier, trying to give off *something* more impressive. More… together.

"My energy?"

He pats the floor beside him.

"Come sit. Let me show you something."

Smashing my hands onto my waist, I hesitate. It's *so* hard to make myself sit beside Jaxon and do nothing.

I'm in work mode. I'm in *chasing-my-future* mode.

"Come on," he urges again.

I sigh hard—surrendering to the inner struggle—and walk over, settling beside him.

"You know, usually—"

"Shhh…" he says gently. "Close your eyes. Feel the stillness."

My mouth stays stuck open. I want to tell him I *get* what he's trying to do. I've *tried* this before. It never worked.

Powering ahead is what worked. Staying busy.

"I have a meeting at nine," I manage to say.

"This won't take long, Zara. You'll see—it'll help."

He places a hand lightly on the small of my back. His voice is soft, coaxing.

"Go ahead. Trust me. Close your eyes."

With a deep sigh, I do it. The sooner this is over, the better.

"Think about everything you have to do today," he says quietly, "and try to arrange the tasks in order —like one giant puzzle. Do it."

There it is. That bossy tone. Even *now*.

Why does it bother me so much?

I squeeze my eyes tighter, trying to dissolve the flare of irritation.

Okay. I need to eat breakfast.

Egg, toast, and coffee before the read—*that's* why this little exercise is so inconvenient.

I sigh sharply.

"Keep going," he says calmly, like he knows *exactly* what that sigh meant.

I roll my eyes—under my lids.

The table read, of course. I'm ready to show the cast and producers they were right to take a chance on me.

Later this afternoon, Jaxon and I are supposed to have dinner in Little Italy. A whole PR stunt.

Paparazzi are in town. Their job is to "catch" us looking cozy. We're not supposed to see them.

Oh—and I have to call Kat before the table read, check if anything new popped up on my schedule or if any urgent calls came in.

That's after I eat. Then table read. Then I'll see.

"Four breaths in, six out," Jaxon whispers.

And somehow, now that my day has a little order to it, those breaths come easier.

Not only that—but my anxiety is gone.

Instead, I feel…

What is this?

I'm not relaxed.

I'm not even invigorated.

I'm in control.

That's it. I'm in control.

"Open your eyes," he says.

And I do.

We're staring at each other.

And—God—I'm smiling.

But he's not.

He's just staring, like he did before rushing out of the theater.

"Zara," he finally whispers, voice thick.

"Hmm?" I'm entranced by the look in his eyes.

He takes my chin between his index finger and thumb.

I blink, hard.

Because in this moment, it feels like a dream—his lips inching closer to mine.

And I'll let him kiss me.

I want it.

I want it *so badly*.

I even close my eyes to receive it.

"Breakfast is in the kitchen," he whispers, his warm breath brushing my mouth.

When I open my eyes, he's staring—holding himself back.

Is this a game?

Is he *teasing* me?

"Was there something on my chin?" I ask, voice echoing through the mostly empty room as I push his fingers away.

And then—he does it.

Jaxon's warm, wet mouth presses into mine.

His tongue sweeps inside, and suddenly my head feels light, like it's drifting off my shoulders.

Our tongues tangle—slow, sensual.

My nipples tighten.

My skin heats.

This is…

"Uh…" he groans, breaking the kiss. "Shit."

I don't know what to do next.

I did *not* imagine this happening today—but now it's happened, and it's thrown everything off.

Or… it *could*, if I let it.

I scramble to my feet.

Straighten my sweats.

Stand tall.

Determined to pretend that kiss—even though it's still echoing through every part of me—*never happened*.

"Um… where's my office?" I ask, dazed.

"Next door," he says, still on the floor, not moving an inch.

I nod.

Then head to the kitchen.

Breakfast. Call with Kat. Table read.

And then…

Oh no.

I'll be alone with Jaxon again.

THIRTY-EIGHT

JAXON WILDE

SEVEN HOURS LATER

It's my off day. Usually, I kick it off—like all my days—with relaxation and setting the day's purpose. Period. That's human stuff. Taking care of myself *as* a human being.

But after kissing Zara?

I've been off.

Why did I do it?

I'm supposed to have more control than that. Is my impulse control getting worse?

Yeah.

It is.

I made sure she was settled in her office before having breakfast. I didn't know what she liked, so I had a whole buffet waiting for her.

She picked one of my egg white omelets and took

a croissant toast with jelly. I didn't think she'd touch any of my three omelets that contain extra protein powder, which I eat to get it all in—but now I'm down to two, and oddly… that's okay.

I like sharing with Zara.

Last night, nearly losing my battle with willpower, I almost knocked on her door to make a proposition.

I can tell she wants me just as much as I want her.

We need to fuck each other out of our systems already.

Just one time. One good time, and we can quit whatever this thing is that makes me want to be inside her *all the time*.

But held out. And also, today, after that kiss, I couldn't do it. I couldn't sit across from her at some restaurant pretending to be on a date. I didn't want to talk to her. I don't want to know anything else about her.

I don't even want an answer to the question that's been gnawing at me: Why did she shoplift face cream? It still makes no damn sense.

Since day one of production, I've been trying to reconcile how someone with her career—her face, her *life*—ends up stealing something that costs less than ten dollars. To me, that's insane.

And that's always been my read on Zara: sexy as hell, but equally off her rocker.

I didn't even want to give her the final pin. But

her team and my team had already ironed out the deal.

Then, Roger said it was the smarter move. He laid out all the reasons why Zara was the safer bet. He's probably choking on those words right now.

Yeah…

I'm supposed to be in Little Italy with Zara—but I flaked.

I had Jen from the team office call her and say there was a team emergency I had to handle.

Anyway…

So how did things get worse?

Earlier, I stood outside her office during the table read—just listening.

The door was closed. Thick wood. Designed to keep the hallway quiet. But I could still faintly hear her.

The way she delivered her lines…

Shit. She's good.

And somehow, that just made things worse by turning me on more. And I hate it.

And that's how I end up here, confessing to Barber, who showed up about three hours ago to meet me for a drink. We're at the green juice bar near the stadium, loading up on nutrients. Two days before a game, we don't get hammered—we get healthy.

"Then why'd you do it?" Barber asks, finishing off his second leafy green Mintastic.

"Honestly?" I lean back, scrub a hand across my

face. "I wanted to know the difference between her acting for real—with lines and shit—and how she acts around *me*."

Barber leans his head back, blinking at me like I just started speaking Cantonese.

"What?" I snap. "That made sense."

It made *performance* sense. But just in case he needs a little more…

"She's an actress."

"So?"

I throw my hands. "So…"

I stop myself before I out myself.

That kiss.

Damn.

She's sweet.

And I can't tell Barber what I've done. That last night—in the shower—I had to relieve the feelings she stirred up.

I want to fuck her from here to next week.

And then—

Barber's gaze shifts over my shoulder.

"Hey," he says, nudging his chin. "Is that the girl from your show?"

I turn fast.

My jaw drops.

Ashley.

Smiling like she's been kissed by today's sunshine, walking toward us.

What the hell is she doing here?

THIRTY-NINE

JAXON WILDE

A lot's going through my head as she bops over, light on her feet. Ashley is the very definition of "bubbly."

The only time I've seen her deviate from that bubbly self was on the reunion stage—when she tried to topple Zara and take her place.

My eyes lock on her tight, shiny pants—second skin. She's also wearing a tight tank top. I bet if she were in Zara's shoes, she'd wear stuff like that around me every day.

We'd have definitely had sex by now. Day one.

"All hail camel toe," Barber murmurs under his breath. "It's all for you."

"Jaxon," Ashley sings, weaving her way through tables.

She initiates the hug we share.

"What are you doing here?" I ask, pulling back.

"I saw you through the window and thought, *Oh my God, it's Jaxon!* I should come say hi. So here I am." She pinches her shoulders up and gives me a little wave, like I'm a puppy.

I grunt. "Hmph."

Force a smile.

Funny thing is—her being here kind of makes me *glad* Anne checkmated us into sticking it out with Zara.

"You wanna sit?" Barber asks, already pulling out a chair.

"Yes," she says, way too brightly.

"So what brings you to San Diego?" I ask.

"Just visiting family."

That smile of hers barely wavers.

"Ah," I say. "You never mentioned having family in San Diego."

"Yes, I did," she says with a soft chuckle, patting my shoulder. Her palm's damp—I can feel it through my T-shirt.

I search my memory for a time she said that. Nothing.

But that doesn't mean she's lying. One of the worst parts of being the show's *Prince Charming* was keeping track of what I said to each woman—and what they said to me.

That show was the hardest thing I've ever done. The women wanted every single ounce of me. But I got it. There was only one of me and, what, nineteen of them?

Zara couldn't care less about being in my company.

And yeah, that bothered me.

Sure, I acted like an ass when I first saw her step out of the limo, but that's because it was weird. She's a well-known actress, for God's sake. I'd even seen her once at a party in West Hollywood.

I don't know why she was there. She looked bored. So I tried to liven things up—said hello.

She looked me up and down like I was scum, then past me like I didn't exist, and walked away.

Honestly, *that's* why I said what I said when she stepped out of the limo.

Petty? Yeah.

But even though she says she forgave me, I don't think she really has.

Anyway. I don't know what to say to Ashley.

"Listen up," Barber says, hopping off his stool with ballet-like grace. "I gotta get back to the old lady."

"Oh," I say. "I'm telling Genesis you called her that."

He points a finger at me. "Bro code, dude."

I nod. Fair.

Barber turns to Ashley. "Nice to meet you," he says, then heads out the door.

I watch him until he's gone, wishing I could follow.

I don't feel right being out in public with another contestant—*especially* after ditching Zara today.

"How are you, Jaxon?" Ashley asks.

I snap my eyes back to her. "I'm fine."

Why does she look so sympathetic? Like I'm in a bad situation with Zara or something.

"I heard you're living with her now?"

Her bright, glassy eyes blink at me like she's waiting for a fairytale confession.

"We're getting close. Splitting our time."

Then I squint at her. "But who told you we were living together?"

It just happened yesterday.

She drops her gaze to the table. "*Top Rag Mag – West* mentioned it."

I grunt, rubbing my chin.

Anne's team must've leaked it.

"Do you ever…" She leans in close, draping her long hair over her shoulder between us. I can feel her body heat. "Do you ever think about me?"

In a million years, I can't picture Zara asking me this question.

None of my exes, either.

And this is why I always had a bad feeling about Ashley. She's just *not* my type.

Even with those tight pants.

Which, by the way, aren't even making *my* pants tight.

"Hey," I say, scooting off my stool. "I gotta go. But—good seeing you."

"Wait."

She grabs my arm—tight, desperate.

Now I'm worried. People are starting to notice us.

"What?" I say, sharper than I mean to.

Her eyes are wide. Almost teary. They dart around my face, searching for something.

I don't want to frown at her. She's a nice girl.

So I make a hard effort to look neutral.

"Don't you miss us?" she asks. "Because I miss you all the time."

I sigh.

I realize now—I have to break her heart.

Thwart her dream of being with me.

Otherwise, she'll never let this go.

"Ashley…"

I gently pull my arm free. "It was just a show. You know that. You signed the NDA too."

I pause.

"I made my choice. And I'm sticking with her."

A beat.

"Goodbye."

And on that note, I get the hell out of there.

That was unsettling.

So much so, I can't wait to see Zara.

FORTY

3 HOURS AGO

Earlier, I was relieved when Jaxon's assistant called to cancel our publicity stunt. After that kiss, we need a break.

I sit at my desk, waiting for the phone to ring. Kat should be calling any minute. I pinch my lower lip. I really liked our kiss. It was so… passionate. But why would I feel all this passion for Jaxon Wilde?

What he said to me after I stepped out of the back of that limousine still bothers me. I said I forgive him, and I do. But I can't forget how low he made me feel. That feeling sticks to me like meat on ribs.

It's funny, though. After the table read—which I slayed—I had this impulse to go for a walk. Not just any kind of walk—the dangerous kind. The kind that led me to that drugstore where I committed theft.

I'm trying to understand why the craving is here. Life is good. But life was also good then.

The abrupt chime of my phone makes me jump slightly. It's Kat. She's always on time. I slide the answer button and put our call on speaker.

"Hi, Kat," I say.

"Hi," she says, but not in a sprightly way. There's a hint of doom in her voice, like she has bad news to deliver.

"Is there anything else I need to be aware of between now and tomorrow's ten a.m. interview with *SLAY* Magazine?" I ask.

"So," she finally says, dragging the word out.

I bristle.

"I received a message from Andrew, who handles your social media. A guy named Trey Morgan DM'd three of your accounts. Does that name ring a bell?"

I steel myself against the discomfort rippling through me. "Yes."

"Okay… do you want to hear more?"

"What does he want?" I ask.

"He says he's your brother. And that Theo is being kept alive by a breathing machine. If you want to say goodbye, you should go see him."

Then, Kat—being the overly competent assistant —says she'll add Trey's number to my contact sheet. I'm still shaking my head. How can I tell her not to do that? I don't want to see Theo in the hospital. Especially when I vowed never to lay eyes on him again.

"Unless you want me to make a call to Trey on your behalf."

"No," I say quickly, then take a settling breath. "Is there anything else?"

"No, that's all," she happily says.

She has no idea the weight of the news she just delivered. Why didn't I just deny knowing Trey like I usually do? Like I do his two sisters.

"Good. Talk to you in the morning."

We end our call with our usual goodbyes, and I remain in my chair, numb on the inside.

I know what I have to do next. There's no fighting the urge.

I need...

FORTY-ONE

1 HOURS LATER

I stand in front of the window of a downtown drugstore. I kept walking until I found a street with light enough foot traffic. That's a sign not many people are inside the store I'm targeting.

This is the perfect place.

And I'm pretty sure nobody recognizes me in my baggy black sweatsuit, with my hair hidden beneath a beanie. I wrapped a scarf around my neck and threw on a pair of fake glasses. It's a sloppy disguise, but it'll do.

The longer I stare at the shelves inside, the more the products blur into memories of Theo.

He's my father.

I lost my mother in a car accident when I was six years old. I was left with him—and he just couldn't raise one damn kid on his own. So he married another woman. Stacy.

Cinderella's stepmother was more loving than she was. She died three years ago of a heart attack. Her loveless heart had finally given out.

For some reason, I turn away from the window and retrace my steps back to Jaxon's apartment. I drop my head in shame as I enter through the garage, just like I had earlier. It feels so... villainous. The amount of effort I put into planning the thrill—snatching something off the shelf, tucking it into my pocket, walking out like it's nothing. Like I got away with it.

Something to put on my face later. Or under my arms.

I've taken deodorant.

As I press the elevator button that'll take me upstairs, I mentally run through the list of other things I've shoplifted. Lipsticks. The scarf I'm wearing. Socks. Bookbags. Pencils. Pens.

Tears fill my eyes.

All the things Stacy bought for her biological children—nice, new. And what did I get? Their hand-me-downs. Their leftovers.

I clutch the left side of my chest as the ache of that memory pierces me.

"Hurry, hurry, hurry," I whisper.

Please don't let Jaxon be home yet. I can't run into him right now.

The elevator doors slide open, and I can barely stay on my feet. I want to collapse. I want to scream so loud the whole world hears me.

I drag myself down the way-too-long hallway. No sound of Jaxon. No trace of his delicious cologne. I keep going until I make it to my bedroom, close the door behind me, strip off everything I'm wearing, and climb into bed.

Now that I'm tucked between crisp sheets and beneath the heavy comforter, I weep.

I see her in my mind. A woman I only remember through photographs—hugging me, kissing my forehead, whispering:

"That's okay, my little pumpkin patch. You'll be fine."

———

A SOFT RATTLE ON THE DOOR WAKES ME.

"Zara?" Jaxon calls gently.

I waver between staying quiet and answering.

"Yeah?" I say, putting on my best voice.

"You okay?" he asks.

"I'm fine."

He goes quiet. I don't think he believes me.

"It's nothing. I'm just tired. Long day. I need sleep."

"Okay... well... um... rest well," he says finally.

"You too," is all I can come up with.

But after Jaxon leaves, I can't rest well. I can't get back to sleep.

What a revelation I had today.

The list of items I've stolen... they were things I wanted so badly when I was a kid.

I need help.

But no one can help me. Not with this. I can't go back and make my dad and stepmother see me. I can't make my half-siblings care that I wasn't treated equally.

Why does Trey think he has the right to message me, as if I should care?

Never.

I'll never lay eyes on my father again.

And after making that vow, I roll onto my side, close my eyes, and finally...

I drift off peacefully.

FORTY-TWO

It's so odd living with someone I haven't seen since Tuesday morning. It's now Thursday afternoon. Jaxon left early Wednesday, and again this morning. According to his schedule, he's been practicing and preparing for tonight's big game.

But the strangest thing happened—yesterday and this morning. When I walked out of my room, someone had left a crystal bowl of those same chocolates that were on my pillow the day I arrived.

It could've been Jaxon.

Or it could've been housekeeping.

I don't know.

Who am I kidding?

It was Jaxon.

It's still hard to reconcile the man I met on the show with the one I kissed and live with. A small part of me wants to dismiss how kind he's being because I fear something might go wrong, but that doesn't apply to the chocolates. I can't resist the creamy, rich milk chocolate—it's irresistible. I've eaten them all.

I considered calling Jaxon to catch up, joke about how we keep missing each other, thank him for the treats and hospitality, but it feels too genuine, and we're just pretending.

The game starts at 5:15 p.m. Today, I plan to redeem myself from Sunday night.

First, there's the outfit: skinny jeans and a football jersey with Jaxon's number on it. A special delivery from Kat arrived this morning with a note saying I should wear it tonight.

That was fine. No complaints.

Next, I wear my hair out—not tucked into a ponytail. I get it now. Those WAGs dress up for their partners. Even way up in the stadium, they want their gladiators to only have eyes for them. My skin is dewy, makeup is fresh but not overdone, and yes—I'm wearing a sweet, expensive perfume.

Then, when I'm ready to go, a car meets me in front of the building and whisks me over to the stadium.

It's show time.

"HELLO," RAY, THE USHER I MET LAST WEEK, CROONS when he sees me.

From the tone of his voice, I've been WAG approved.

The scene is set. It's one of the best days of my life. I'm happy and excited to be one of the special girls.

"How are you?" I say cheerily.

"All is good," Ray says, flashing nearly all his teeth.

We make small talk. He tells me it's a full house tonight. He says he's lucky to work at the stadium where he can watch the game for free.

"It's a difficult lineup for Jax tonight with Ray..." He taps himself on the chest. "My name. Robson." His satisfied smile widens. "But Jax should beat him."

Then he launches into all the reasons he thinks "Jax" is worthy of the jersey I'm wearing. He uses words like *spin*, *stiff arm*, *cutback*, and *elude*.

Jaxon actually showed me all those moves the other day. Pulling from the index file in my brain, I kind of understand the lingo now.

I thank Ray for getting me to the private suite safely.

"Any time, Zara. Any time," he says before traipsing off.

Now it's time for my final grade.

I walk to the open-air section of the suite, where the ambiance of game day is alive and buzzing. Their eyes are on me. Genesis, at first, looks annoyed as the same lady from Sunday night escorts me to my seat. I notice her eyes travel up and down my outfit. I even have on strappy sandals with heels—even though it's chilly tonight. But I'm already winning because I'm confident she approves.

When I settle into the seat beside her, she's still looking me in the face like my mere presence irritates her.

"Hello," she finally says.

I smile. "Hi," I say.

And my smile isn't fake. I like Genesis. I find her loyal—to the team, to the culture, to all the stuff happening tonight from the center of the field to the highest corner of this venue.

And she's saucy, in a very real way.

I get it. She thinks I disrespected their universe.

On Sunday night, I had.

But tonight?

I'll show her.

FORTY-THREE

I'm on my feet, jumping up and down beside Genesis.

I'm sure she doesn't realize what she's doing, but she's squeezing the heck out of my arm while Jaxon—ball tucked tight under his arm, perfectly guarding it—runs like a cheetah.

It's impressive. Ray was right. Ray Robson, number forty-seven, has been sticking to Jaxon like glue, but Jaxon manages to evade him. He's running so fast.

I'm screaming so loud my brain feels like it's going to explode.

Then, Ray Robson gets his hands on him, hoists himself on top, and slams Jaxon to the ground.

I press my hand over my thundering heart until— thank God—Jaxon leaps to his feet and tosses the ball to the referee. He's up, and now I can jump up and down with Genesis without fear.

Especially when the Jumbotron reveals that Jaxon just ran twenty-seven yards, setting the team up for a fresh round of four more downs.

Genesis nudges me with her elbow, her eyes still glued to the field. "He's going to score," she says.

"And I'm awake this time," I say.

She actually laughs at my joke. Thank God.

"You're into it. What changed?" she asks.

"Jaxon taught me the game."

She involuntarily looks at me, missing the snapping of the ball. I want to match her eyes, but I keep mine locked on the field. I want to see this happen.

And it does.

Micah Jameson, the quarterback, throws the ball so fast, with such intensity, that I lose sight of it—until Jaxon reaches for it and dives into the end zone.

I'm up again, screaming my head off, hugging Genesis.

And when I look up at the Jumbotron to see how Jaxon is celebrating, he's looking up too—smiling.

Of course they capture a shot of me. The sleeping girlfriend isn't napping tonight.

But I want to do something extra special. Not for show.

For Jaxon.

So I raise my thumb—high and happy.

And he sees it.

He raises his thumb back.

A FUNNY THING HAPPENS: TATI, WIFE OF A RIGHT tackle named Josh Banks, includes me in the round of tequila shots she buys for all the girls.

That's what they call each other—*the girls*—and I think, as of tonight, they consider me part of the crew.

Jaxon scores two more times, and each time, we do the thumbs-up thing. I hope he doesn't think I'm pretending. I can't wait to tell him that I meant it. He's the reason I'm really enjoying the game tonight. So, yeah—not only is he playing like a demigod, but he's made it possible for me to enjoy *him*. And for that alone, he deserves a thumbs up.

There's less than a minute left. San Diego has the ball and is up by only three, even though Jaxon scored three times. I'm chewing on my nails, but Genesis, Onetra, Tati, and everybody else isn't.

"Don't stress, honey," Genesis says, patting my arm. "They're going to run out the clock. We won."

"Oh," I say, exhaling the tension from my body.

Then she leans in and says, "Come with us tonight. We're throwing a little after-game party."

My mouth drops. I mean, I knew I was making inroads with the girls, but a *party*?

"Are you serious?" I finally ask, totally shocked.

"Yes, honey. It'll be fun."

My stomach does little dances, and my heart skips a beat.

Is this what it feels like to be one of the girls? Like, for real?

Because on the show—I faked it. I fake-bonded with the girls. I can admit that now. No wonder they all dumped me in the end. I didn't know how to be real with them.

But I can feel it now.

Genesis and the girls... they could end up being my friends.

For real.

FORTY-FOUR

Genesis and Barber's home is nestled high on a hill. It's huge—mansion-sized—with sweeping windows and three sprawling floors. She drove me here in her very expensive half-sport, half-luxury car with cream-colored leather seats and high-end everything. The whole thing smelled like wealth and newness.

She's rich. *Very* rich. And on the drive over, I learned Barber's salary isn't the only reason why.

Genesis was a hedge fund analyst before marrying him. As she whipped through San Diego's winding hills, she casually mentioned that she'd quadrupled his paychecks—and that when his contract ends, he could retire at twenty-eight.

"But he loves the game too much," she said with a shrug. "Still, we made a deal: if we ever see signs of brain injury, he quits. Through our private provider, we scan his brain three times a year."

I was stunned. The same woman who once told me our job was to "eat, sleep, and breathe our football players" had actually taken an *industrious* approach to that idea. I'd assumed she meant keeping him happy so he didn't stray. But no—Genesis is playing chess while the rest of us are learning the rules.

You never truly know someone until you *know* them. I'm learning that more and more these days— starting with Jaxon.

Inside the house, the vibe is casual luxury. There's a spread of sliders, truffle fries, lobster corn dogs, and steak crostini with truffle butter—just a few of my new favorite things. I haven't eaten all day, and I had one strong tequila shot, so this food is a godsend.

Only women and children are present for now. Some teenagers are night-swimming, while younger kids are wrangled by nannies as their mothers sip cocktails and socialize.

Onetra and Tati—who sat in the same section as me in the suite earlier—have claimed the end of the largest sectional I've ever seen and waved me over. I heard this room isn't even their living room. It's designated for "events." Casual.

"So," Onetra says, "how's it going with Jaxon?"

Her question is vague enough to be polite but clear enough to say she's interested. I can appreciate the finesse.

"Things are humming along nicely," I reply, keeping it short and sweet.

"And you're staying in San Diego while working in L.A.? You're still acting, right?" Tati adds.

"I'm between projects," I say, giving them another neat, non-revealing answer.

But they're still watching me—nodding, smiling. I can feel it. They're wondering why I'm so guarded. What's my deal? They're not even digging deep, just asking the basics. Surface-level stuff.

So I open the door a little.

"However," I say, watching their eyes spark with curiosity. "I start a new TV show in about three months, so I'll be back and forth prepping for that."

"Oh, how exciting," Tati beams. Then she leans forward, placing both hands on my knee. "You know, I used to watch you on *Emergency*. You were my favorite character. I was *so* happy when Jaxon chose you."

My jaw drops a little. I didn't expect that.

"Oh—well, thank you."

"But…" Her face shifts, and I already know what's coming. "You know. The stealing…"

"Don't," Onetra cuts in, shooting her a look.

Tati winces. "Too far?"

I think about that. She asked the question, but under the surface, she's asking something else: *Are you safe to be real with?*

So I give her real.

"No," I say easily. "Yes, I stole the face cream. And I'm just now starting to understand why."

"Did they make you go to rehab?" she asks, softer now.

"Actually, yeah. For two weeks."

"Did it work?"

Onetra groans. "Don't ask her that! Zara, you don't have to answer her nosy-ass questions."

"I wasn't being nosy," Tati protests. "I'm just curious. I want us to be friends. She's… real. Like, not a dainty eater. She throws down."

I burst out laughing. "Oh, I'll be hitting Pilates hard next week," I joke, holding up a half-eaten lobster corn dog.

Our laughter shifts the energy, and the conversation moves on to Onetra ranting about how Chris Liles still hasn't proposed.

"If Jaxon marries you first, I'm going to kill Chris," she says dramatically.

"Well…" I stand, dusting off my lap. "Jaxon and I are just beginning, so I don't see Chris in an early grave quite yet." I wink.

Onetra offers a pensive smile and launches back into her rant with Tati as I slip away toward the bar, where I order a tonic with lemon.

"Onetra and Tati cornered you?" Genesis appears at my side.

I flinch slightly—didn't hear her coming—but keep it cool. "Yeah. But it wasn't that bad."

She raises a skeptical brow. "Wait… Are you drinking soda?"

I raise my glass. "I like my calories to be funner than alcohol. Like this." I take a bite of the lobster dog.

"Aren't they *so* good?" she says, eyes twinkling as we both scan the room.

It's still mostly women. Music's playing. The vibe is alive, but relaxed.

"This gathering just for the girls?" I ask.

But before she can answer, I see them: a wave of tall, athletic men pouring into the room. One of them locks eyes with me—and I with him.

It's Jaxon.

FORTY-FIVE

It's been two days since I've seen Jaxon this close in person. Sure, I watched him on the field. I saw his image flash across the Jumbotron. We exchanged thumbs-up signals. But now, standing here under soft lighting, with his eyes locked on mine, it hits differently.

This moment feels… perfect.

As he walks toward me, I instinctively think to suck in my stomach, fix my hair, adjust my posture—anything to look just a bit more *together*. More attractive. This is the part where the boyfriend greets his girlfriend, right? Even if it's pretend.

Across the room, a few heads turn. One woman nudges another, whispering as they both glance my way. I shouldn't care. I tell myself this is for the cameras, for the illusion. But my pulse flutters like it's prom night. Jaxon's eyes haven't left mine. And in this room full of people, it somehow feels like it's just the two of us.

Finally, we're face-to-face, and I have to tilt my head back to meet his gaze.

"Wow, congratulations," he says, beaming. "You got an invitation."

My face warms as I glance down, a chuckle catching in my throat. Then it dawns on me.

"Wait... were you planning to come without me?"

He points toward the food table. "Have you *seen* that spread?"

I burst out laughing. "That's fair. I would've come without you too."

We laugh together—real and easy—and for a second, I forget everything else.

"How you been?" he asks once the laughter fades.

The memory flashes—me curled up in bed two nights ago, not answering his knock on the door. The weight in my chest returns. But I hold his gaze and keep my voice light.

"I've been fine."

His head tilts, a subtle sign that he doesn't quite believe me.

I press my lips together, considering whether to tell him the truth. Not about the store, not yet. But about my father. About Trey. About everything bubbling under the surface. But this moment—this place—feels too public. Too exposed.

"So," he says, his tongue sweeping briefly across

his bottom lip. God, he has the most beautiful mouth. "I have to kiss you. They're all watching, waiting for proof that this is real."

My breath catches, and heat coils in my belly. The flutter in my chest turns wild.

"Are you okay with that?" he asks softly.

"Mm-hmm." I nod, head light, nerves buzzing.

Jaxon steps forward, curling one strong arm around my waist and drawing me in. I rise onto my toes, but he lifts me off the floor with ease, holding me tight against the strength of his body.

God, he's so hard… and in all the right places.

Our eyes lock.

This is the scene.

My role.

The—

His lips crash into mine, silencing every thought. His mouth is urgent, his tongue swirling around mine —tasting me, claiming me. He's needy, but I match it with equal hunger. The world around us fades to a blur.

Even when he pulls back, lips breathless, my body is still humming, alive with electricity.

Warm breath brushes my ear as he whispers, "Let's get out of here."

FORTY-SIX

"No way you're leaving," one of Jaxon's teammates says, hooking an arm around his neck and dragging him away from me.

I don't know the guy's name, but his eyes are already glossy—the first signs of being three sheets to the wind.

Jaxon and I hold each other's gaze, full of longing. My body's still cooling off from our make-out session.

I'll be back, he mouths.

But I doubt it. He disappears with his teammate into the crowd and doesn't look back.

I feel stripped bare, my want for Jaxon slathered all over me. Everyone can see it, and what makes me feel so exposed is that I've lost the upper hand. What we just did wasn't fake. Not even a little. My heart might actually be on the line now.

Slowly, I turn my attention to the room. Nearly everyone's watching me. Some are smiling—happy, it seems, to see the "TV couple" looking legit. Others look surprised, maybe even skeptical, their expressions sharp with gossip.

I am an actress. I like attention.

But not all attention is wanted.

Seeking refuge from the curious, whispering onlookers, I lower my head and make my way to the food table. At the very least, I can get another lobster dog—the most addictive thing I've ever eaten.

As I take a few blissful bites in peace, planning to work the room again and get to know more of the ladies, a woman I haven't seen before steps up beside me—way too close. She stares at the spread like she's on a mission to find something specific.

"I suggest one of these," I offer, holding up my lobster dog.

"Oh no," she says, smiling. "Those'll have you up in the middle of the night *fiending*."

We both laugh.

"By the way, I'm Lindsay. Everybody calls me Linds. Jake Ruff's wife. He's a linebacker."

I extend a hand. "Zara Morgan."

"I know who you are," she says, shaking my hand. "And congrats on taming the dog."

Mid-bite, I freeze. "Huh?"

"Jaxon's been… *the ladies' man*." She says it in a faux-announcer voice, clearly for effect.

My eyes narrow slightly. I think she's trying to rattle me.

"Haven't they all?" I reply coolly.

She doesn't like that. Her tiny face scrunches into a sour expression.

"Not *my* husband," she says, patting her chest, clearly offended.

Okay. So she's one of those.

I'm not used to this kind of nonsense in real life—people walking up to me, starting petty drama like it's their full-time job.

Then she leans in closer, glancing over both shoulders.

"Anyway," she says, lowering her voice, "I thought you and Jaxon weren't really a thing."

My eyes widen slightly. I don't even know how to respond without losing my cool.

"But if it is…" She raises her hands, bracelets and rings clinking. "My bad. I just thought… you did something to him a while back."

My chin lifts. "I did what?"

"At a party when he was a rookie. Blew him off or something. He told Jake he'd never forgive you for that."

I open my mouth, stunned. I had never seen Jaxon before I stepped out of that limo. What is this girl even talking about?

And why now? Why bring this up after the perfect moment we just shared?

"Is there anything else you want to get off your chest?" I ask, voice calm but laced with steel.

She blinks, then closes her eyes and exhales, almost repentantly. "Sorry, I just heard myself." She steps closer. "If I were you, I'd want to know all of it. I've seen so many girls get hurt by these guys. They've got options—and a lot of them don't know how to say no.

"I don't know what changed between Jaxon claiming he couldn't stand you until now, but... just be careful." Then, breezily she adds, "And you know what? I think I will have the lobster dog."

She plucks one from the platter and takes a bite, like she didn't just drop a verbal bomb.

I'm momentarily paralyzed, sorting through it all.

"You're right," I finally say. "I would want to know."

"Good," she replies, already walking off.

FORTY-SEVEN

JAXONE WILDE

I get it. Tonight, we get to loosen up a bit. Tomorrow, we're hitting the road to Jacksonville, where we'll start training at our new facility on Saturday. After that, we're heading to Denver to train in the altitude and get our lungs ready for game day.

Usually, I'm the life of the party on nights like this. No holds barred. We get plastered. Pretty girls wall-to-wall. The cheerleaders should be here soon—those who like to hang out, anyway. Not all of them do.

"So, um… Jax…" Jake hooks his arm around the back of my neck and slides something small into my hand. A folded piece of paper.

"This is from Rachael. Says she misses you."

Rachael. One of the cheerleaders I kicked it with for a hot minute last season. Casual, nothing serious.

We fizzled without a word—no drama, no breakup. At least I thought.

I look at the note but don't unfold it. Jake's watching me too closely. So is Rob, standing just behind him like he's waiting to see how I'll play this.

I slip the note into my coat pocket.

I'll throw it away later.

"That's it?" Jake asks.

"I have a girlfriend," I say.

Jake tilts his chin and narrows his eyes, one brow cocked like he's auditioning for doubt. That look pisses me off more than his question.

"I have a girlfriend," I repeat, firmer this time.

"Yeah, but… come on. Sticky fingers?"

The heat rises in my neck. "Don't call her that."

"She's hot. I get it. I would, you know… myself. But brother, she's Hollywood, playing a fucking part. She fell asleep during your first touchdown," Jake adds with a smirk, like he's trying to bait me.

I look at him, then at Rob, both of them waiting for me to slip up.

"Not only that," Rob chimes in. "She's too much of a distraction."

I snort. "I scored three times tonight."

"Yeah, but not last Sunday," Rob fires back. "You had buttery fingers, man."

"Fuck you," I mutter. "Zara is my girlfriend, and she's not going the fuck anywhere. So get over your jealousy already. And you know what?" — I button my coat — "I'm leaving."

I storm out. They call after me, voices softening, pretending they were just messing around.

But fuck that.

Let them drink and laugh and talk shit. I've got better places to be. I've got Zara. And I need to finish what we started earlier.

FORTY-EIGHT

It's quiet between us as Jaxon drives us back to his place. He's pensive, just like me. I find the silence advantageous—I need it to think about what Lindsay said. Her delivery sucked, no doubt about it. But she's right. I should be careful.

That doesn't mean keeping what I learned tonight to myself.

My body hasn't changed its mind. Every cell still wants to experience an old-fashioned Jaxon Wilde ravishing. Yet, my heart and head want me to pump the brakes—at least until I gain some clarity.

I shuffle through my memory, trying to locate a party where I ran into Jaxon during his rookie year. Nothing surfaces.

I shift uncomfortably against the leather seat. The material is so soft and supple, it doesn't even scrunch.

"Everything okay?" Jaxon asks.

I perk up a bit—he's given me a gateway into the conversation I need to have.

"Did we ever run into each other at a party during your rookie year?" I ask, keeping my eyes pinned on him, determined not to miss the smallest reaction.

Jaxon stares out at the road ahead. His Adam's apple bobs, and somehow, he suddenly looks years younger—maybe reliving some rejection I can't recall.

"Who told you that?" he asks.

"A woman named Lindsay. One of your team-mates' wives. I can't remember his name."

"Jake," he says, rubbing one side of his face.

"Then… is it true? Because I honestly don't remember it."

He snorts, almost bitterly. "I guess I wasn't memo-rable enough."

Whoa. He sounds hurt.

"No," I say quickly, firmly. "That's not why I wouldn't remember you, Jaxon."

He stiffens at the correction.

"It doesn't matter," he mutters. "That was eight, nine years ago."

"But it does matter. I want you to understand—that was when my career was just starting. Anne had just signed me. She attached a PR rep to get me 'out there,' present me as a fresh new face rising toward stardom. It was the most uncomfortable period of my life. Well… second to the reality dating show."

Finally, Jaxon glances over at me. His expression is softer now.

"Anyway, I had this weird, exhausting schedule of parties I had to attend—meet the right producers, actors, directors. So if I ran into you at one of those events... I wasn't really there. Nothing mattered except the people I was assigned to connect with. I'd show up, smile, say the right things, and leave."

The ick from that period washes over me, and I shiver.

"It's the part of this business I hate. You know?"

The car turns onto the driveway in front of the building.

"We'll valet tonight," he says as the vehicle comes to a stop. "Stay seated."

Not able to look away from him, I nod. I think he's accepted my explanation. But I still haven't done the one thing he accused me of being incapable of: seeing him.

Before he can hop out, I reach for his arm. My fingertips rest there, just long enough to make him pause. Jaxon likes doing this—opening doors for me. Being old-fashioned in ways that are surprisingly endearing.

"I'm sorry," I say quietly. "If I was rude back then... I didn't mean to be. I used to dissociate sometimes when I got nervous. That version of me... she didn't know how to carry herself. Being an actress taught me how to interact with people. I'm better now."

He stares at me, unreadable. It's his turn to say something.

But instead, without a word, Jaxon slips out of the SUV.

My door opens moments later. He takes my hand and helps me down, tossing his keys to the valet, who cheers after catching them like he's just won a prize.

It's as if we're in our own universe, together, hand in hand, as we stroll across the lobby, all eyes on us—some cellphones even pointed in our direction.

For the first time, it all feels like an unfair intrusion into our privacy. I'm relieved when we make it to our private elevator.

He touches the security plate, and the door slides smoothly open.

Normally, he waits for me to enter first, but this time he grips my hand tighter and walks in ahead, gently tugging me along.

Our bodies fall into rhythm. Jaxon maneuvers me until I'm backed against the mirrored wall. My feet leave the floor, and I'm wrapped in his strength, our breathing deep and matching.

His eyes melt into mine, holding me there.

"Thank you," he whispers, voice low and rough.

"For what?"

"For explaining why I wasn't good enough for you.

Because you are a magnificently beautiful woman, Zara."

I've never felt that—*truly felt that*—until this very moment. Even as my faith begins to fade, I feel seen. And wanted.

The elevator dings, but Jaxon doesn't move.

"This is the third time we've been in an elevator together," he says. His crooked smile hints at what he's about to do.

I glance around him, concerned the doors might close again and take us back down.

"Relax." His grip tightens. "They're on sensors."

Without warning, he claims my mouth, devouring me in a kiss that is all hunger and heat. Our tongues meet, soft, slick, and slow, and my knees weaken. I moan into his mouth, his taste flooding me.

His hand slides between us, fingers pressing into my center through the thin fabric of my pants. He circles me there, slow at first, then faster, applying just the right amount of pressure.

I gasp.

"I can't wait to taste you," he growls against my lips.

Then, in one smooth motion, he unbuttons my jeans, unzips them, and pushes his hand inside.

"Step out of these," he murmurs—*commands*, really.

Normally, that tone would trigger a reaction in

me, but this time, it sends a pulse of pleasure through my entire body.

I obey.

He lowers me just long enough for me to step out of my pants and panties, then he lifts me again, his hands full of my hips. His mouth melts over my cilt. So soft, so…

"Ha!"

FORTY-NINE

I cry out again—loud, unrestrained, undone. My legs tremble, too weak to hold me up after my third orgasm in a row. But Jaxon, relentless in his mission to pleasure me beyond reason, sweeps me into his arms and carries me out of the elevator, leaving my pants and panties behind like forgotten casualties of lust.

We can't stop kissing. Our mouths find each other again and again as he carries me, and I feel as light as air in his arms. He's solid, sculpted muscle wrapped around steel—every inch of him driving me wild. I'm touching everything I can: his neck, his jaw, his shoulders, the line of his collarbone. But I need more. I need his skin on mine. I need *all* of him.

By the time we're in his bedroom, I'm seconds from begging.

This isn't my first time in here. I have entered

without his permission this morning, snooping, of course. But everything feels different now. The room is black leather and chrome, white and black marble floors. It's masculine, modern—and wildly erotic. A den built for sex.

Jaxon lays me across the bed and begins to strip. First his pants. Then his shirt. And when he stands before me, naked, fully revealed, I nearly combust.

"Off with your shirt," he commands, voice hoarse.

I obey instantly.

My hands move to the clasp between my breasts.

"Leave it on," he adds, eyes dark, low-lidded, heavy with lust.

I freeze, my fingers releasing the clasp as I raise both hands in surrender. His control only inflames me more.

"Now spread 'em," he says roughly. "I want to see what you've got for me."

I part my thighs slowly, shamelessly. I'm soaked—*dripping*, and I know he sees it. My body is weeping for him, begging to be filled.

Jaxon groans, his gaze devouring me. He's hard—*so hard*—but he doesn't move an inch closer. He just stands at the edge of the bed, watching me like he's memorizing every curve, every breath.

Finally, his eyes meet mine.

"What is it?" I ask, starting to rise.

"Don't," he says sharply. "Don't move."

I freeze.

But I'm suddenly unsure. "Is everything okay?"

He's breathing harder now, chest rising and falling. "I just need to say this."

He pauses. Swallows. Then—

"If I take you… you're mine. Not fake. Not public persona. Mine—for real. Got it?"

A long ache pulls through me. My whole body pulses with the want of him. I nod—fast, hungry, desperate.

That's all he needs.

Jaxon moves over me like a storm. My hands spread across his chest—warm, firm, perfect. His skin is satin over stone, and I melt beneath him.

Then I'm on my back, his weight heavy on top of me, grounding me, surrounding me.

And then—*finally*—he enters me.

He stretches me open, slowly, deliberately.

He thrusts.

I gasp.

I moan.

I am *full* of Jaxon Wilde.

We are no longer fake.

We are real—here, now, in every thrust, every breath, every inch of this wild, breathless, all-consuming moment.

FIFTY

The sun is up, and Jaxon and I haven't slept a wink. We still can't keep our limbs—or mouths—to ourselves. He's gone down on me so many times I've lost count. Each time, his tongue laps my clit with precision, taking me from zero to one hundred in a matter of seconds.

And don't get me started on when he finally unclipped my bra—ceremoniously, like it was some kind of sacred act—and sank both my breasts into his warm, greedy mouth. The way he used his tongue and teeth? It was like every nerve in my nipples had been lit on fire.

The man is... highly skilled.

The sheets on his bed got so soaked that after my legs gave out—again—he carried me to another room. All white. Hotel-chic. Five-star everything.

That's where we are now, tangled in each other, his lips on the bare skin of my back.

"Shit," he murmurs, pressing a kiss to my shoulder. "I'm gonna sleep straight through the flight to Jacksonville. And the rest of the day. Without you." There's frustration in his voice—because this has to end soon. Two weeks apart might as well be forever.

I flip over, needing to see his face. His *stupidly gorgeous* face. I kiss him again, drunk on his mouth, but have to pull back before I float right into unconsciousness.

So we just lie there, eyes locked, exhausted but unwilling to close the space between sleep and goodbye.

"Can I ask you something?" he finally says.

I raise a brow, nodding.

"The other night, when I came to your door… You'd been crying, hadn't you?"

The question hits harder than I expect. It brings it all back—the weight I'd shoved down.

"Yes," I whisper.

"The kiss didn't upset you?"

"No," I breathe, kissing him softly. "It was... family shit."

His eyes flash with concern. "What kind of family shit?"

"My father," I say. "He's on life support. On a breathing machine."

Jaxon immediately props himself up like he's ready to call someone, fix something.

I place both hands on his chest—my favorite chest—and press him gently back down. "It's okay. I'm not close to him. Or his family."

His brow furrows. "His family?"

I nod. "My mom died when I was six. Car accident. My dad couldn't handle me on his own, so he remarried. She hated me. Treated me like I was a burden. And he just... let her. So yeah. We're not close."

Jaxon looks at me like he's trying to rewrite the story in his head—change the ending, offer comfort with just his eyes.

For a second, I wonder if I've said too much. I've learned the hard way that not everyone wants a partner with family baggage. It makes people wonder if you're damaged, incapable of being a good mother or wife.

Maybe he's rethinking everything.

"Hey," he says, gently tapping my chin. "Come back."

I blink. I hadn't realized I'd drifted into a spiral.

"All families have their shit," he says softly.

I exhale, shoulders loosening. "What about yours?"

He smiles. "Three sisters. Which is why I'd never hurt a woman. Ever."

Then his attention shifts—his eyes drift downward.

"Yes," he murmurs with a grin.

"What?" I ask, following his gaze.

Oh.

Oh.

He's hard again. Ridiculously so.

"I'll take it nice and slow," he promises, crawling over me like a man who knows exactly how to ruin a girl in the best possible way.

"Yeah," I breathe, my legs parting automatically as he glides into me.

We're both sex-sore, stretched thin with want—but this time is different. This isn't about frenzy. It's about finishing what we started—one last time.

Before the two-week drought begins.

FIFTY-ONE

2 DAYS LATER

I loved the convenience and luxury of Jaxon's place—but it's nice to be home, back in my soaking tub.

It's been a long day, one I kept full on purpose—mostly reading through scripts from movies and shows in case *Next In Line* falls through. Fingers crossed it never does. That's exactly what I told Jaxon.

He chuckled in solidarity. We're on our second call of the day. This morning, he called to make sure I got home safe, driving his SUV. He insisted I take it. I was supposed to leave yesterday, but I told Kat to turn the car around and send the driver back to L.A. I ended up sleeping the entire day in Jaxon's bed. I was wiped.

"Oh, and I've been thinking," I say, something

from the drive home bubbling up again. "Remember that comment you made about the ladies watching their figures?"

"Yeah," he groans. "And you tore me a new one. But I didn't mean it the way you thought."

I let out a soft laugh. "I know that now. Especially now that I've gotten to know you better. When you said you had three sisters—it all clicked. You *make* sense."

"I do?" He sounds amused—and kind of pleased.

"I know how we women are. We obsess over our weight, our looks…"

"Yes!" he says, like I just won a game show. He tells me how nearly every day, one of his sisters would ask, *Do I look fat in this?* And to him, they never did. As an athlete, he says, too skinny means too weak.

"I was just trying to connect with the women," he says, "and I said something stupid. I regretted it the second it left my mouth. You had the right reaction."

I adjust the phone against my ear. "Nah, I could've been kinder."

"We've learned our lessons, haven't we?"

His ability to forgive—gently and with humor—hits me straight in the chest. I had assumed the worst about him back then. Now I know how wrong I was.

Gosh, am I falling in love with Jaxon Wilde? Or is it just the sex talking?

"Hey," he says softly.

"Yeah…" I purr back.

"Umm…" He groans a little. "I miss you. But I've gotta go—game day tomorrow. You watching?"

I smile so wide it actually hurts. "You better believe it."

"Good. Be on the lookout for our signal on the Jumbotron."

"I will," I promise.

We say goodnight. There's a pause. One of those long, lingering silences that's *this close* to becoming a confession. But I won't say it. And I'm pretty sure Jaxon thinks it's too soon, too.

So instead, I say, "See you tomorrow."

"Goodnight," he says again.

"Goodnight."

As always, he waits for *me* to hang up first. Jaxon Wilde—a true gentleman.

Phone still in hand, I stare at the screen, caught up in the warmth of our call. I want to tell him how I feel. Just… see what he does with it.

I type:

> I think I love you.

But I delete it.
I try again:

> I think I'm falling for you.

I let it sit there. Read it over. And over.

The truth? I've already fallen.

No. No, no way. If deep down Jaxon's a commitment-phobe, even *that* might scare him off.

So, I delete the message. Set my phone down.

And stare into the depths of my bathwater, willing all these messy, impulsive declarations to disappear.

FIFTY-TWO

JAXON WILDE (270)

GAME DAY

I'm not going to lie—it's been tough.

Not one, not two, not even three—but *four* beautifully thrown passes have gone straight through my hands.

Coach has benched me. It's the right call. I'm winded. I'm slow. My head's not in the game.

I was afraid this might happen. But it's not Zara's fault—it's mine. I didn't ground myself since Thursday morning. I didn't run my sprints. Didn't go through my drills. And now, I'm paying for it.

But there's something else, too—something I can't name. I'm playing more cautiously than usual. And I don't understand why.

"You're playing like shit," Jake says, flopping down next to me on the bench.

"If that's all you came over here to say, then get the hell up and go back to where you were." I'm in no mood for one of his passive-aggressive Zara comments. He's had it out for her since day one.

"And so are you, by the way," I add. "They're handling you like a ragdoll."

"Ha," he scoffs, spitting aggressively on the grass. "Don't do that to me, man. We're down by fourteen, and we rely on your consistency to win. You know that."

I clench my jaw. He's not wrong.

He pats my arm. "Get it together. Figure it out. But I'm not sure if it's the actress or the runner-up. Look."

He nods up toward the stands.

I look.

And I freeze.

Ashley.

What the hell is *Ashley* doing here?

And then, like some kind of twisted magic trick, the Jumbotron lights up with a side-by-side of me and her. Overhead text reads:

THE FINAL PLAY

What the actual fuck?

"Look at you, Jax," Roland Tucks shouts, running backward to line up. "All the baddies came out to see you."

I flip him off.

"Get your head in the game!" he yells back.

I stare a second longer, stunned. Ashley's presence here is like a glitch in the simulation. She *could* be stalking me. It wouldn't be the first time someone's done that. But *this?* The Jumbotron graphic?

Someone set this up.

Before I can unpack it, the announcer calls: "3rd and 8."

Our defense has been holding the line hard—if it weren't for them, we'd already have an "L" next to our name.

"Jax in!" Coach shouts.

I shoot to my feet. I know exactly what I need to do.

Play to the same level as our defense. Forget about Ashley. Stop craving Zara. Shut the noise out, and do my damn job.

I'm running. Roaring. Gnashing my teeth like an animal.

I'm going to put twenty-one on the board before this game is over—*at least.*

FIFTY-THREE

TWO DAYS LATER

I can't stop staring at my phone.

It's on the table, and I'm willing it to ring— or ding—with the special sound I assigned Jaxon's texts. I haven't heard from him since Saturday night.

I didn't catch the game. I had to attend the annual party at the studio producing *Next In Line*. There was no getting around it. I *had* to be there.

I'm glad I went, though… because I got a surprise. One that's still got me shaken to my core.

Which is why I'm here with Anne at the café in her office building. She only has an hour, and I'm taking all of it.

"I don't know anymore," I say, swirling my straw

in my iced coffee. "Blaine and I—on the same show. How did this even happen?"

Anne gives me *that* look. The one I hate. Her sneaky look. The one that says she's been holding out on me because she thinks she knows what's best.

"What is it?" I ask sharply.

She sighs. "Okay. Let me just put all the chips on the table."

I slap the tabletop. "All of them."

"Blaine's the one who recommended you for the role of Kayla Norton."

My stomach drops.

She holds up a hand before I can speak. "And I jumped on that shit, Zara. You were a sinking ship."

I wince. I felt it when I saw him last night—*that* feeling. Like I'd been kicked in the chest. And now, hearing this?

Anne was there when I couldn't get out of bed. She doesn't know about the shoplifting, but I have a closet full of crap I took when Blaine made me feel like nothing. Like I didn't matter.

And now he's back? Hand-delivering my career on a silver platter?

I glance at my phone again and shake my head. What the hell am I doing wrong in life? Why do the people I trust always end up slicing the deepest?

Blaine hadn't shown up to table reads—his character comes in at episode three as Peter Folks, a cousin with a legit claim to the family's empire. But last night, his smirk told me *everything*. He knew I was shocked. Knew I was pissed. And he enjoyed every second.

He never apologized for cheating on me. Just slipped straight into victim mode. *I* was the problem. *I* needed help.

But last night it hit me: Blaine isn't living life—he's producing *The Blaine Show*. And I'm just one of the characters.

The way he looked at me... then pretended not to. The way he *tried* not to stare at every beautiful woman in the room—like he was putting on this whole show just for my benefit, like he wanted me to *notice* that he wasn't looking. That fake restraint, that forced composure—it was the biggest tell of all. He hadn't changed. He was just trying harder to *look like* he had.

And now I'm scared.

Am I doomed to fall for Blaine Bello types? All romantic and attentive at first, then disrespectful—and dangerous—by the end?

I mean... I had to go to the doctor. Get tested for everything. Thank God there was nothing I couldn't cure.

Anne's voice is running in the background, something about professionalism and power. About putting on my "big girl panties."

Yes. She actually says that.

Then she frowns. "Why do you keep looking at your phone?"

I blink. "What?"

She narrows an eye. "You know you're doing it."

Before I can respond, *her* phone dings—not mine.

Her brow furrows as she checks the screen.

Then her whole face tightens.

"What the hell is this?"

She turns her phone around.

It's a video from the Jumbotron—**a split screen of Jaxon and Ashley**. She's blowing him a kiss.

My jaw drops. My throat tightens. Tears crowd my ducts, but I won't let them fall. Not here. Not now.

"I gotta go," I mutter, frantically grabbing my purse and jacket.

Anne grabs my arm. "Zara, take a beat."

I freeze.

Too late. The tears are slipping out.

"Oh no," she whispers, finally seeing it. "I *knew* this would happen. I *knew* Jaxon liked you."

She lets go of my arm, but her gaze holds me in place. "And you like him too. That's clear. So…"

She folds her arms, eyes narrowing with fresh calculation. "Have you been waiting for him to call you?"

I nod, ashamed. "Yes."

Anne thinks for a moment. "This—we can't

have." She stands. "Zara, this is about your career. You're *here*—on the precipice. Millions of people have come to this city chasing what you have. Do *not* let boys ruin what you've built with your talent. Got it?"

I look at her—really look. Petite. Pretty. Looks like she belongs in a Hallmark movie. But she's tough. Ruthless, even.

She once told me she didn't start out this way. But "this business is full of sharks. And if you don't bite first, they'll eat you alive—blood, guts, and all."

Still, she *loves* the art. The artists. That's why she's stuck with me. She believes in my talent.

She's the one person in the world I trust the most.

So I bite back the tears. Screw Jaxon and his SUV —I'll have Kat arrange for someone to return it today.

Anne taps the table. "I need to hear you say you got it."

"Yeah," I say, voice small. "I got it."

She points at me. "Don't do anything stupid. If he calls, don't answer. If he texts, don't answer. I have to fix this. Got that too?"

I nod.

She studies me like she's still not sure she can trust me.

Then finally: "Hang in there, Zar." She winks— and disappears like she's off to fight a five-alarm fire.

I just sit there. Numb. Thinking.

We haven't even *touched* the Blaine situation yet, but right now? That's the lesser issue.

Blaine, I can ignore.

But Jaxon?

What the hell am I supposed to do about *Jaxon*?

FIFTY-FOUR

Kat arranged for someone to pick up Jaxon's SUV and drive it back to his place within the hour. I'm doing a final sweep, making sure I haven't left anything behind. That's when I spot his coat on the seat. A real duster coat. Like a man.

I stare at it, wondering if it's hiding anything.

There's a voice in my head: *Be careful what you look for.*

I try to shake off the warning and reach into one of the pockets.

My fingers brush something—folded paper. My stomach knots. I hesitate.

Is this wrong?

Should I just leave it?

But my grip tightens. *Screw it,* I whisper, and pull it out.

A yellow Post-it, folded into a square.

I unfold it and read the handwritten words:

Meet me in the same room as last time. I'm waiting. —Rach

I wish I couldn't believe my eyes. But I can.

I don't know when Jaxon received this note from "Rach." But he wore this coat the night of the after-game party. Was Rach one of the women there?

"Um, hello?"

A deep male voice from behind makes me jump out of my skin.

I whirl around, heart pounding.

A man stands there. Older. Familiar.

I slap a hand over my chest, trying to steady my pulse.

I know that face. He looks like Theo. My dad.

"Trey?" I breathe, my eyes darting toward the open gate. I left it ajar for the driver who should be arriving soon.

"What are you doing here?" I ask, though it feels like I'm floating outside my body.

"Can we talk?" he says.

I blink hard. I don't know if I want him to disappear—or if I'm actually glad he's here.

"Sure," I say finally. "Follow me."

I fold the note and keep it, then place Jaxon's coat back on the seat exactly how I found it.

My feet barely touch the ground as I lead Trey—my brother, seven years younger—into my house.

FIFTY-FIVE

I offered Trey coffee, tea, water—or even a glass of wine if he needed it for whatever this is we're about to do—but he declined everything.

Now he's made himself small on my sofa. He must be twenty-four, maybe twenty-five. He's nervous, that much is clear.

"Okay," I say, settling into the armchair across from him. "What are you doing here?"

I want to ask how he even knows where I live, but I don't want to sound rude. After all, he's my brother.

"You didn't answer our calls because... well, you have us blocked."

He says it like the words are scraping his throat on the way out.

I don't move. Because he's right. And up until this moment, I've never felt even an ounce of guilt about it. But seeing him here—wearing a surprisingly stylish jacket that pairs well with his black chinos—makes me feel… strange. Maybe even regretful. I don't know.

Suddenly, he scoots to the edge of the sofa.

"Listen… I've always wanted to say this to you. I believe people are shades of gray. No one's just one thing all the time. But my mother… she was the exception. She was one thing, most of the time— actually, all of the time."

He pauses, watching me. Reading me. If he could hear my thoughts, he'd hear silence.

I'm confused. I expected him to defend her, to paint her as misunderstood. But that's not what this is.

"I can count on one hand the number of times my mother didn't act like a narcissist," he says quietly. "Did you know she almost drowned me in the tub when I was a baby?"

He's watching me closely now—like he's waited years to say this, and even longer to hear my response.

I shake my head slowly. "No. I didn't know that. I knew you were gone a lot during your first few years. I'd ask, 'Where's the baby?' and Theo would say you were at your grandmother's house. I thought…"

I close my eyes as a wave of old, buried sadness floods me. I can't believe I'm about to say this.

"I thought she didn't want the baby around me… because I would enjoy it too much." My voice trembles, which annoys me. I don't want to sound weak.

Trey stares. And I stare back.

It's wild how much we resemble each other. We

both favor Theo more than our mothers. Though I see traces of my mother in me, I see none of Stacy in Trey.

"If you had stuck around—though I completely understand why you left—I think you'd know… our experience with her was different. But not better. Just… different. You know?"

I lean back, stunned. "Wait—she tried to drown you?" Because that revelation has just sunk in deep enough.

His jaw tightens. "Yeah. She said she had post-partum depression. Maybe she did. Maybe she had it her whole life."

He rubs his eyes. "I don't mean to speak ill of her. She was my mother. I had to love her. But… she was—"

"Abusive," I say.

"Abusive," he echoes.

The room suddenly feels too small, like the air's been sucked out of it.

"We hated it," he says. "Me, Linda, Bloom… we all hated it. The way she treated you. I want you to know that. Not everything my mother did was delib-erate—she couldn't help herself. She needed help, but she never got it. And it took Dad a long time to realize that."

I sigh, feeling heavy all over—mostly inside.

"I don't know why you're telling me this," I say.

"Because our dad is dying. And he loves you. He

misses you. And you can't let him leave this world carrying that guilt. You just can't, Zara."

I drop my head, eyes closed. Little Trey is sitting here with a big ask.

Forgive Theo? For letting his second wife treat me like a second-class citizen in my own home?

"I want to show you something, if you don't mind," Trey says gently, cutting through my spiraling thoughts.

I lift my head, glaring now. Thankfully, I'm not crying. I'm too angry for tears.

"What?" I snap.

"I had a conversation with our father before he got worse. It was about you. I recorded it without him knowing. And I want to show it to you."

IT'S LATER. TREY HAS GONE HOME WITH A MAYBE from me. Maybe I'll go see him soon—maybe. I have too much going on right now. I need to think about what I'd even say.

My father looked nothing like the man I remembered. He was thin, small, all skin and bones. Seeing him that way broke my heart. Because my dad was not mean. He was slow to anger, which was the problem. He should've been angry at Stacy. But at least now I know that he was—and why he never expressed it.

Trey asked him, "Dad, if you knew how my mother was, why did you stay with her? And have two more kids?"

At first I thought my father was so far gone that he didn't comprehend Trey's question. But then his lips trembled before he spoke.

"When Wilamina died, it all came crashing down on me. I thought I would be with her for the rest of my life. I wanted to die too. But I had… Zara."

My dad went silent for a long time. Trey remained patiently still.

"I didn't think I could do it alone," my dad said. "Marrying Stacy was my biggest regret—and the best thing—because I love you kids. I worked a lot. I didn't pay attention. I figured, she was like Wila. Soft and beautiful and kind. But… that was me not facing the truth. I want to tell her I'm sorry."

"Who, Dad?" Trey asked.

"Zara. She got the worst of it. She was gone before I finally stood up to her."

"Yeah, and she left."

"And then she died," my dad said.

Their silence loomed, and I thought that was the end until my dad finally added, "I was scared to be a single father, and that's on me. Zara doesn't have to forgive me. I haven't earned her forgiveness."

And that was the end.

I asked Trey something I hadn't cared to know—until now. "What happened to him?"

"He caught pneumonia and then while being treated in the hospital, it turned to sepsis."

That answer, more than any other, is what finally gets me out of bed.

I open my laptop and email Kat.

FIFTY-SIX

FRIDAY

It's three days before Jaxon's next game. I've gone the entire week without obsessing over how heartbroken he left me. That's a win. I've been hurt by a man before, and I'll probably be hurt again—many times before it's all over. So, I'm gutting it up. Feeling the sadness, mourning what could've been between me and Jaxon, and moving on.

The good news? I've been in constant communication with my brother Trey—and even Bloom, my twenty-two-year-old sister. We've decided to put our father under my health insurance through The Guild. Yesterday, he was transferred to one of the best hospitals in the world.

"He's already improving," Trey says, his voice breathy with movement. He's rushing between classes.

He's in the MFT program at USC. Being a fixer suits him, and oddly, I like him a lot. I like my sisters too.

We've spent hours on the phone talking about surviving their mother. I listened mostly, slowly realizing I was never alone. We've all agreed to move forward—together.

I haven't seen my dad yet. He's still in critical care, and they want to limit exposure to any new germs. I hope he makes it. I really do.

"That's excellent," I say.

"So, we'll talk soon?" he asks.

He always finds a reason to call—little things, big things, it doesn't matter. I think he's afraid of losing touch again. And honestly? I get it. I don't want to lose this connection either.

With that, we end our call, knowing we'll speak again sometime this weekend.

The sun dips low over the ocean, golden light flickering across my desk. I sit at my computer, absently sliding my finger across the top of the keyboard.

Here's the thing—if I truly want to get over a man I shouldn't have fallen for in the first place, I need to go full masochist. I have to make it hurt more.

So, I search: *Jaxon Wilde + Ashley Sweet*. If that's even her real name. I've fully accepted her little Disney character voice, and fragility is probably an act.

It doesn't take long to find something. There's a

video of them at a juice bar in downtown San Diego. The timestamp says it was his off-day—the very day someone from the team's office called me and said he couldn't make our commitment because he had prep work. We were supposed to be photographed together in Little Italy.

But here he is. With her.

"He lied," I whisper, shaking my head.

He's been playing me all along.

I exhale what feels like every last bit of air in my lungs. I close the browser. I don't need to see more. Ashley at the game. A secret meeting with "Rach." A full day with Ashley. And then, an entire night with me.

His stamina is impressive. His integrity? Not so much.

"Jeez," I mutter. "I'm going to need another gyno appointment."

"Fuck!" I shout loud enough to miss my phone buzzing at first.

My heart jumps—until I realize it's not Jaxon's ringtone. I should delete that custom tone already.

I flip my phone. The name on the screen makes me groan.

"Ugh," I grunt.

I consider sending it to voicemail. But no—I'm sick of letting men treat me like a damn ping-pong ball.

I answer. "What do you want?"

"Hey," Blaine croons, smooth as ever, like there's no bad blood between us.

I want to scream. But I don't. I pull up the imaginary zipper on my big-girl panties.

"What do you want, Blaine?"

"Toby… Toby Lane."

I squint. What?

"I wanted to make sure you're okay with me being on the show. Did, um, Anne tell you everything?"

Look at him, acting like getting me cast on the show was some grand gesture I owe him for.

I decide to play along—this is business, not forgiveness. Blaine's a liability in designer shoes, and if I don't manage him, he'll poison the set. We're not friends. We never were. And I'll make damn sure he never forgets it.

"No, but hey… let's have a drink, and you can tell me everything," I say lightly.

He hesitates a second too long. Then: "Sure. When?"

He's too eager. He thinks I'm a fool.

"Tomorrow night," I say. I need time to plan.

"Deal."

We hang up after I promise to text him the time and place.

Then I make another call. To someone I need to pull this off.

FIFTY-SEVEN

SATURDAY AFTERNOON

I chose a restaurant Blaine and I used to frequent when we were a couple. There are dozens of paparazzi shots of us canoodling in quiet corners or dining on the patio—smiling, holding hands, pretending to be in love. We knew we were being watched. We lived for it.

I benefited the most from being Toby Lane's girlfriend, though I never realized it until last night. Back then, I wanted the relationship to last forever—even though it rarely satisfied me. It was a romance built as much on PR strategy as it was on affection. And it worked. For both of us.

I fully expected Blaine to show up late. Instead, he's already here. Thankfully, I made a reservation or he might've chosen a seat hidden from the cameras.

But I made sure he'd be in full view. He's seated by the front window. I timed our "date" perfectly—5:30 p.m.—early enough for soft, golden sunlight to flood the glass, but late enough to imply intimacy. This is the kind of dinner that the press assumes ends in a shared car ride and tangled sheets.

Blaine looks up from his phone and waves. I strut slowly toward him, giving him time to take in every inch of me in this gold, short, sleeveless Roberto Cavalli. I bought it years ago, after my first big check, when designer labels meant something to me. Blaine used to love when I dressed like this. Sexy. Flashy. Compliant.

Now, I just feel like a beautifully wrapped decoy. I hate this dress. It isn't me. It never was.

Back then, I was constantly shoving my square self into all of Blaine's round holes.

When I sit across from him, grinning too wide, blinking too slow, gazing at him like he's the sun—I realize something so simple it almost makes me laugh:

I never loved him.

I didn't even like him.

"You look hot as hell. You sure you don't want to order and take it all to go?" he croons.

I gesture to myself. "And waste this outfit? No."

It takes him a second to chuckle. I think he really wanted me to say yes. Would the old me have thrown away a night out just to rush home and have sex? Maybe… Okay, fine. Yes.

Yikes.

"So Blaine, how's it been?" I ask, launching the small talk.

He hates this question, always has. And he proves it again—just shrugs and grunts like that somehow answers it.

"Not good?" I press, because I never used to.

"Not bad," he says.

"So not good and not bad?"

His eyes narrow. He's already irritated. I have to rein it in—remember the optics. We're supposed to look like we're reconnecting. Not sparring.

"All good. Not bad," he finally settles on.

"Excellent." I deliver the line like a toast, and he grins again, settling back into his smug comfort zone.

He lifts his chin. "Did you wear that for me?"

"It kills me to say this," I reply sweetly, "but I did."

His eyes light up like a fool who thinks he's still got it. "That makes me hopeful, because…" He leans in, rubbing his palms together like some dime-store villain. "I did it all for you," he whispers. "I couldn't watch you go down. I love you too much."

Zara, do not burst out laughing. Hold. It. In.

My eyes widen with faux emotion. I thought pretending to be Jaxon's girlfriend was the role of a lifetime—but no, it's *this*. Right here.

I reach across the table and take Blaine's hand. I know exactly how much he hates being the one passively held. His masculinity is made of wet tissue paper—can't get too damp or it falls apart.

Right on cue, he adjusts our grip, making sure he's doing the holding. Perfect. Vera, I hope you got that shot.

"Well," I say lightly, "it's a great gig. I love the script. Couldn't put it down."

Blaine leans back, basking in the credit. "That's what I do. I look out for people who... look out for me."

Finally. There it is.

I chuckle like he just told the best joke of the year.

Another one for the camera, Vera.

"Come here," I say, curling my finger to beckon him closer. I let our faces hover inches apart—cheeks nearly touching, breath mingling, the press-ready illusion of a kiss.

"I want to show you something," I whisper. "I call it..." I pause, lick my bottom lip—watch him practically pant. "An attitude adjuster."

Snap, Vera. Get the damn money shot.

We both pull back at the same time. The moment's over. Now we get to the real show.

I slide a small stack of folded pages from my purse and lay them out on the table like a poker player going all in.

"See this?" I tap one of the pages. "These are my lab results. See the part that says I needed meds? Now look who my only sexual partner was at the time."

He scoffs, eyes narrowing.

The waitress appears, bouncing over like she's ready for a casting call. Pretty, flirty—probably an aspiring actress. Usually, Blaine would flirt back, slip her his number on the receipt, then come back later and sleep with her. But tonight? He doesn't even look at her.

"We need a moment," I say.

She gives him one last desperate smile before retreating.

"You're disgusting for this," he finally mutters.

"I agree. I mean, what would your fans think?" I ask, all innocence. "Their heartthrob gave his girlfriend the clap? No wonder she shoplifts—look at the man she loved."

Blaine shakes his head, growling, "What do you want?"

"Peace," I say. "That's it. We work in peace." I lean forward and press my finger down on the paper between us. "And I don't owe you a thing. If anything... you owed me.

FIFTY-EIGHT

JAXON WILDE

GAME DAY

Up early. Power breakfast. Team meeting to finalize the game plan. Now it's time to hit the field for warm-ups.

I've forced my head back into the game. I can't play like I did last Sunday—slow, distracted, off. Tonight, I have to shine. I *have* to put multiple scores on the board.

Even better? Next week is our Bye Week. No field, no travel, no pressure until two Sundays from now. That gives me one shot—to go out big and shut everybody up.

But none of that matters if I can't lock down the one thing still eating me alive.

Zara.

I've been completely cut off—no phone, no

laptop, no way to reach her. And not just her. *Anyone.* It's driving me insane.

I still don't trust Roger, and I'd bet money he's the reason my phone vanished. But Anne Park? She's another problem altogether.

The moment I realized I was stranded on the road with no way to communicate, I had to get crafty. While waiting to board our charter from Florida to Denver, I grabbed one of the gate agents and asked for help.

He tracked down Anne Park's number. Her assistant patched me through.

I explained everything.

"Tell Zara I want her at Sunday's game," I said. "I'll have a seat saved for her. Please just ask her to come."

"Mm-hm," Anne replied, vague and cold. "Talk soon. Gotta go." *Click.*

That was Wednesday.

Since then? Silence.

None of the guys will lend me their phones. They're pissed about Sunday, and in their minds, my game went downhill the second Zara stepped into the picture.

Sure, I dropped the ball early—but when I pulled it together, I scored one and ran over a hundred yards, helping us pull out a win by a single field goal. We're now three and zero.

But they're playing this superstition hard—like if I

stay out of contact with her, we'll break a team record and secure our first ever four and zero season start.

As we jog toward the field to stretch out, Jake appears at my side. He's watching something on his phone.

"Oh, shit," he mutters. "You gotta see this, Jax."

He tries to hand me the screen.

I scoff. "Now you'll let me touch your phone?"

"Just take it," he insists, pushing it into my chest.

I should throw it back at him. Better yet, bolt with it and call Anne again. But it's Sunday—she's not at the agency.

What's happening to me now is a solid case for not relying on contact lists and actually committing phone numbers to memory.

If only I had remembered Zara's number.

I take the phone. What's on screen stops me cold.

It's one of those dumb gossip roundup videos. But this one's a knife to the gut.

It's Zara. Dressed like fire. Her lips are inches from Blaine fucking Bello's.

I shove the phone back into Jake's hand, jaw clenched so tight my teeth ache.

"Why'd you show me that bullshit?" I snarl.

Jake says nothing.

I walk off, stomach twisted, heart somewhere in my shoes. I feel worse than I did last Sunday.

Way worse.

FIFTY-NINE

Why am I even watching this stupid game?

I guess because I'm curious. I want to see if the Jumbotron will catch Ashley in the stadium, playing a better version of the devoted girl-friend to Jaxon Wilde than I ever could. If she's there, then it's confirmed—Jaxon's replaced me with the runner-up.

So far, there's been no sign of Ashley, but maybe that's just because the game's barely begun—and Jaxon is playing terribly.

I winced when he dropped what looked like a perfectly thrown pass. From what Jaxon taught me, the ball landed right in his "pocket." He should've caught it and run for another first down.

Instead, the Bull Sharks are now forced to kick from centerfield.

"This is not good for the Bull Sharks," one of the excitable announcers says.

"No shit, Sherlock," I mutter.

These guys talk too much.

That's why I mute them.

My doorbell rings.

Half-distracted, I leap off the couch and dash to answer it. I've been waiting for Kat to bring over a fresh, secure copy of *Next In Line* episode two's script. According to Steven—one of the show's creators and lead writer—I must guard it with my life.

As soon as I swing the door open, I'm met with Kat's warm smile.

I really like her. She's such a boss—a woman who puts her head down, gets things done, never complains, and handles every task—large or small— like it's mission-critical.

"Hey, you," I say, lit up with anticipation as she hands over the packet.

I nearly snatch it from her fingers.

"You want to come in? I'm having a little private party."

Her eyebrows rise curiously, and her smile answers for her—she's in.

"I'm watching Jaxon's game," I admit with an eye roll, feeling like a low-key troll in my own living room. "Don't tell anybody."

"Your secret's safe with me," she says, shrugging off her thin jacket as she steps inside.

She follows me to the living room and eyes my indulgent spread—Filet-O-Fish sandwiches stacked like a fast-food Jenga tower, steak fries, and a bottle of wine.

Kat gives me a look: chin lowered, eyebrows raised, a gentle scold in her expression.

Yeah. I know.

"I'll be okay with workouts and walking," I say defensively, reclaiming my seat. "I just needed a day of indulgence."

Especially after yesterday's showdown with Blaine... and today's game, which feels like the final nail in whatever Jaxon and I were—real or fake.

"I get it," Kat says, grabbing one of the Filet-O-Fish sandwiches.

She sits a little stiffly, still unsure how casual she's allowed to be around me.

"How about a glass of wine?" I offer, hoping it'll help her loosen up.

She glances over her shoulder like someone's there to give her permission.

"Well... okay," she says. "Just one glass. I'm driving."

I race to the kitchen to grab another wine glass.

"Are you going to turn the volume back up?" Kat calls out.

"If we must!" I reply with faux cheer.

As soon as the announcers come back on, one of

them says, *"And there's Ashley Sweet today, supporting Jaxon Wilde."*

"That's what she says," the other quips. *"But I'm not sure how much her support is helping."*

Thank God I don't have one of those open-concept kitchens. I wanted separation between my rooms—because right now, I need it. Kat can't see me stop short, gripping the counter, blinking back the sting in my eyes.

I won't cry over this. I won't.

Jaxon played me. Got what he wanted—me in his bed—and moved on to the runner-up, all while pretending I was the prize.

Asshole.

I inhale deep, straighten my spine, square my shoulders.

If Kat weren't here, I'd change the channel. Probably cue up Netflix and lose myself in a show where men don't lie. But this show must go on.

I paste on a smile. "Here comes your glass!" I call out, chipper as hell.

And I step back into the room, ready to finish the scene.

SIXTY

"Oh… wow!" Kat shouts at the television.

I've gasped, my hand still clamped over my open mouth.

Jaxon just got smacked in the head with the ball. His arms flailed like windmills, but his hands never touched it. It was like watching a scene from a slapstick comedy.

Then the Jumbotron cuts to Ashley, who's hugging some girl she came with—looking oh-so-distraught. But what grabs me isn't her Oscar-worthy performance—it's Genesis, in the row behind her, glaring down with a bitter grimace. And before the camera cuts away, Genesis rolls her eyes.

Yay, Genesis! She really is my friend.

"Did you see that?" I say to Kat, pointing wildly at the screen.

She doesn't answer.

I turn and look at her. She's sitting stiffly, her face a shade redder than usual. There's something she wants to say, but I can tell she's hesitant—like she doesn't want to overstep. I get it. I'm her boss. It's smart to tread lightly.

So I decide to dial it down. No more theatrics. No more flipping out over a guy.

"I'm surprised they're leaving Jaxon Wilde in," one of the announcers says.

"That's Tibbey's style," the other responds. "He doesn't mind losing a game. He wants Jaxon to play through it. Get over it."

"Well, it's going to cost them the game if Jameson keeps throwing to him," the other chimes in. "Seems like Wilde's got distractions."

Kat erupts. "You see these guys? It's always a woman's fault when a man falls apart. That's bullshit. A man doesn't make me bad at my job. So why is it her fault if he's playing like shit? That means he's mentally weak. And it's not even…"

I turn to her, startled. That's the most personal thing I've ever heard Kat say—and it has nothing to do with logistics, scheduling, or production.

"Touché," I say quietly, even though it sounds like I'm defending Ashley. "You're right. It's not her fault."

Kat narrows one eye, lips pressed tight. I frown. Something's off. But then I hear the announcer say, *"Third and ten,"* and I spin back to the screen.

The snap.

Micah Jameson is well-covered and scrambling. He lobs it—and this time, Jaxon actually catches it.

But he's hit—hard.

The ball flies out as he crashes into the grass. One of his teammates recovers it, thank God, but Jaxon stays down. He's rolling, gripping his ankle.

I jump to my feet, heart in my throat. "Oh no. Oh my God."

I glance at the door, then toward my room, already thinking—*I need to get to him.*

But the Jumbotron flashes Ashley again. She's hugging her friend, her eyes big and glassy.

Right. *She's* his person now.

I slowly sit back down. "He's not my problem anymore."

"No. Don't sit," Kat says.

I turn to her. She sighs and slumps her shoulders.

"If I tell you this," she says, "you can't tell Anne. I mean it. She'll fire me."

Her voice is shaky, but her eyes are dead serious.

I get it. I might be her boss, but Anne is a barracuda—merciless and meticulous. If Kat crosses her, she'll be shredded. And at this stage in my barely blossoming career, there's not much I can do to stop it.

"I won't say anything," I promise.

Kat leans forward. "Jaxon couldn't find his phone. Anne knows Roger arranged for someone to take it. But he found a way to call her. On Wednesday."

My brows lift.

"He told Anne everything. Said he wanted you at the game. Asked her to tell you. I think… I think that's why the seat next to Genesis Cartwright is empty."

She pauses.

"It's your seat, Zara."

My heart squeezes.

Kat looks at me and finishes, "So… don't sit down. You know what you have to do."

SIXTY-ONE

Kat managed to book me a charter flight through a company in her personal Rolodex—from Burbank to Denver. I threw together an overnight bag, and she drove me to the airport herself. While I sat on the tarmac waiting to take off, I called Genesis. She promised to keep my arrival a secret from her husband and pick me up at the airport.

Before we left, Jaxon had been carried off the field on a stretcher. The announcers speculated something might be broken. I hope not.

This flight feels endless. I keep checking the time on my phone, even though it's on airplane mode.

"Prepare for landing," the captain finally announces.

I exhale, releasing just a little of the tension I've been holding since takeoff.

I'm halfway down the ramp when a flurry of delayed messages flood my phone. Both Kat and Genesis confirm the same thing: Jaxon may have a broken leg.

I spot Genesis standing by the back of a black Town Car with tinted windows, waving at me.

"Broken leg?" I ask as my feet hit the asphalt.

"Might," Genesis says.

The driver takes my bag and slides it into the trunk.

"That's the worst scenario, but nobody knows yet," Genesis mutters. "Hurry—we have to get to the hospital. She's there."

She raises her hands like claws, mimicking something grotesque.

No need to ask who she's talking about.

"*She's* at the hospital?" I say as I slide into the back seat beside her and buckle up. The thought is almost too pathetic to entertain—especially now, knowing what I know.

"*She's* in the waiting room, pacing around like she's his damn wife. I don't get it. I *know* he's into you. So what the hell is going on?"

I tell her everything—what Kat revealed, how Jaxon lost access to his phone, how he managed to get a message through Anne, and how I suspect Ashley's been showing up to games thanks to an inside hand giving her those seats.

"What the actual hell?" Genesis growls, shaking her head. "I *cannot* believe Barber went along with taking his phone. I swear, I'm going to rip into him."

I place a hand gently on her shoulder. I'm grateful she's in my corner. It's comforting in a way I didn't know I needed.

"Don't yell at him," I say. "The team's gotta do what the team's gotta do. I think they believe Jaxon's been underperforming because of... women drama."

She scoffs. "Please. That makes zero sense. You're our friend—and so is Jaxon. And whatever strategy they think they're using clearly isn't working. He played like *shit* today. The last time he was his old self? You were there. How do they *not* see that?" She throws up her hands. "Idiots. And Roger? Useless. All ego. I should have his job."

The car pulls up in front of the hospital entrance, and without delay, we're out and moving fast. Genesis knows exactly where she's going. I thank my lucky stars I landed on her good side. There's no way I'd be getting to Jaxon this smoothly without her—and, of course, Kat.

But then—

Cameras start clicking. Flashes pop.

A small pool of media has been cordoned off in one section of the lobby, but they see me the moment we walk in.

"Zara Morgan!" a few of them shout.

And then the questions start flying:

Are you here for Jaxon?

Are the rumors true?

Is your relationship fake?

I bow my head, and both Genesis and I pick up the pace. Thankfully, the elevators are just ahead.

We're almost there when, from a quieter direction behind us, a woman squeals, "It's Agent Laura Merton!" The name of my former character on the hit television show *Emergency*.

I turn just in time to see the fan clap both hands over her mouth, eyes wide and starstruck—like she might cry, or scream, or rush me for an autograph.

That's when I spot someone else trailing behind her.

Ashley Sweet—more cunning than sweet.

She's holding a coffee cup like she's been pulling an emotional all-nighter: frazzled, wrecked, devoted. Playing the perfect girlfriend part.

But that look on her face? She's more than startled to see me—she's not thrilled I'm here now.

SIXTY-TWO

shley and I both glance at the open elevator like it's a race to see who'll reach Jaxon's floor first. Cameras are still clicking. Flashes still popping.

"Go ahead, sign the autograph. I'll keep the elevator open," Genesis says, moving to hold the doors.

Ashley checks over her shoulder like she's considering an escape—then straightens her posture and saunters past me into the elevator. She seems confident. Too confident.

Is it possible she and Jaxon have worked something out?

Oh my God... that stunt I pulled with Blaine.

Had Jaxon seen it?

Am I too late?

"I'm Caroline," the woman says, tugging my attention back.

I quickly scribble: *Thanks for your support. I truly appreciate it.* Then I sign my name.

"I hope they bring you back," Caroline says.

"I'm tired of waiting. Can we please go up and send it back down to her?" Ashley calls from inside the elevator. Her syrupy tone has thinned out—less sweet, more sour. That fake charm? It fooled me once. Not anymore.

Just then, the elevator next to hers opens—and lo and behold, Jaxon's inside. On crutches. And he's not alone.

"Sure! Go on up!" I say quickly, nodding like mad.

For a split second, Genesis is frozen, but I think she follows Caroline's line of sight. She slips into the elevator and slams the *up* button just in time to close the doors. Ashley probably caught on at the last second—but it was too late.

Roger spots me before Jaxon does. He looks like he's chewing lemons. His whole body jolts, like he wants to stop what's about to happen—

But then Jaxon and I lock eyes.

SIXTY-THREE

JAXON WILDE

Everything shifts the second I see her.

The pain in my leg, the fractured fibula, the weeks of recovery ahead—they all fade, if only a little. She's here. And that's what matters.

"No." Roger's hand presses against my chest to stop me from moving. "We're going back up."

I push past him. "What the hell is wrong with you?"

While I lay in the hospital bed earlier, waiting for confirmation on the injury, I had time to think. To retrace how I went from the peace of being with Zara before we left for Florida to feeling like I was unraveling on the field. Everything had changed too quickly. Too quietly. And now I know why.

Ashley showing up at both games. Sitting in prime seats—the kind that cost tens of thousands… or are arranged by someone with power. That didn't happen by accident.

Then Roger walked into my room, pretending to be surprised that Ashley was around. He showed me the tabloid photos of Zara and Toby. Said maybe I should lean into the story, let people think I was moving on too. He had comments printed out—actual fan commentary, like their opinions were enough to steer my life. According to him, Zara and I were a sinking ship, and Ashley was the obvious next chapter.

That's when I knew for certain that it was all planned. All of it orchestrated by him.

I kept my jaw clenched, trying to keep my temper in check. "I want my phone," I told him.

He didn't deny anything. Just reached into his pocket and handed it to me like we were swapping business cards. The battery was drained—completely dead.

He knew what he was doing.

"Here's the deal," he said calmly. "Ashley's here, and so is the media. You're going to do a press conference. Tell them it's over with Zara. Say you and Ashley are figuring things out. That's all. Then we're done with her, and with that agent of hers."

I stared daggers at him. That was the real issue. Anne Park. He couldn't stand the fact that someone outsmarted him. That she had won.

I told him I didn't want to see Ashley until we got back to San Diego.

He didn't respond, but I could see it in his face—he was already planning his next move.

I had plans too. A press conference wasn't going to go how he thought it would.

But none of that compares to what just happened.

"Hi," Zara says. Her voice is quiet, uncertain. She lifts her hand slightly, like she's not sure if she should even be here.

I make my way toward her, trying not to move too fast on the crutches. Every step hurts, but I don't care. She's here.

"I'm sorry," I say. "About everything."

She frowns, surprised.

"I know Anne didn't pass along your message. And I don't know if you saw the photos of me and Toby, but none of that was real. I'll explain later."

I release a sigh of relief that I didn't know I was holding.

Roger's voice cuts through behind us. "Let's go."

He's already heading down the hall with the press following him. They're snapping photos of us now, like this is part of the story too.

I glance at him briefly, then turn back to Zara. I don't want to waste another second.

"It feels like it's been forever," I say.

She nods, her eyes soft. "I feel the same way. It's been... hard." Her voice wavers, just enough to crack.

Her skin looks impossibly soft. Every nerve in my body remembers her—how she felt wrapped around me, bare skin to bare skin, the heat of her, the way she pulled me deeper and deeper inside her.

"Can I kiss you?" I ask, my voice low, the words catching in my throat as I swallow—bracing for whatever comes next.

She doesn't answer—she just leans in.

Our lips meet, and something in me settles. Her hands on my face, my hands at her waist. The crutches fall to the floor, and I don't even care. The pain in my leg pulses, but it barely registers.

All I feel is her.

Her mouth. Her breath. The warmth of her body leaning into mine. The moment we lost, the weeks of silence, all of it disappears.

She's here now.

And so am I.

SIXTY-FOUR

I help Jaxon steady himself on his crutches.

"Stay by my side," he says in that bossy tone I used to hate—but now it makes me hot.

As we head toward the press room, a breathy but unmistakable, "Jaxon?" floats after us. We both turn. Ashley is trotting toward him.

"Grab my shirt," Jaxon murmurs to me. "Don't let go."

He turns away from her without hesitation, walking forward even as she flanks him, clinging like this is her last shot at claiming the man she thinks belongs to her.

I glance at her keeping pace, determined, unwilling to let go.

Inside the press room, cameras start flashing immediately—capturing the three of us like we're in some warped love triangle finale.

A staff member reaches for my arm. "Please, have a seat..."

"She's with me," Jaxon says without breaking stride. Then, thumbing behind him, adds, "She's not."

We continue down the center aisle between two packed rows of reporters. At the front, Roger leaps to block us.

"Move," Jaxon says, low and commanding.

"No." Roger folds his arms, puffing up like he's ready for a showdown.

It happens fast—Jaxon stiff-arms him, sending him tumbling over the front row. As Roger scrambles to regain his footing, Jaxon is already at the table, pulling out the lone chair behind the mic setup.

"We need another chair up here," he tells someone nearby.

"No, this is not happening!" Roger barks.

But Coach Tibbey steps between them. "Sit down, Roger."

The tension spikes. They lock eyes. But Roger obeys, slumping into a seat with visible resentment.

Camera clicks fill the room, capturing every moment. Jaxon slides his hand under the table and takes mine.

When I glance at him, seeking reassurance, he leans over and kisses me—a quick, decisive kiss—and every camera shifts focus.

He leans into the microphone.

"You all know Zara Morgan, right?" he says.

A few scattered voices respond: "Yes."

"Well… Zara Morgan is the woman I chose. I'm her Prince Charming. Isn't that what the show was all about?"

He flashes that smile I've tried to pretend I didn't love. That dimple? It's deadly. I once swore it annoyed me. But when we made love, I kissed his face so much my lips should've left a permanent imprint.

"And I figured something out while we were on the road," Jaxon continues. "I was playing like—well, not great. And it's because we hadn't made this real. Official. Locked in." He turns to me. I'm already smiling.

"I love you," he says. "Probably have since day one."

A loud voice bursts from the back of the room.

"He's lying!" It's Ashley.

Heads turn.

"They're not a real couple!" she shouts. "I have proof!"

"Get her out of here," Jaxon says into the mic.

"I have proof!" she screams again as security begins escorting her out.

She keeps ranting as they carry her off, babbling about how he should be with her, how I'm fake—until finally, her voice fades.

Now all eyes are back on us.

"I love him too," I say into the mic. "For real."

"And…" Jaxon adds, "Keep watching us. If we're lying, you'll know."

A surge of questions erupts.

"One at a time!" he calls out.

A reporter rises above the noise. "Jaxon, what do you say about today's performance? What happened out there?"

Jaxon nods thoughtfully. "I played terribly. Then I got hurt. But…" He jerks his thumb toward me and grins. "She's my lucky charm, and she knows it."

He leans back and drops it in his Terminator voice: "I'll be back."

The room erupts with laughter.

SIXTY-FIVE

We flew back to San Diego together. With the medication kicking in, Jaxon slept through most of the flight. Tomorrow, his rehab begins at the team's facility.

It's just been the two of us. I carried his crutches while airport staff rolled him down the ramp and out to our waiting car. Of course, everyone had their cellphones pointed at us. I guess this is how it'll be now—us, a "celebrity couple."

It's strange. We were pushed together by the spotlight, but now that we're real—truly a couple—it feels more personal than ever, even as the world watches. But public fascination is like a flickering match—it flares, then fades. The longer we're together, the less interesting we'll be to them. I honestly can't wait for that part.

When we got home, I helped Jaxon into the

shower—he definitely needed it. I took mine after, planning to give him space for the night so he could rest and get comfortable. But he asked me to stay close. I wanted that too.

Earlier, we fell asleep on opposite sides of the bed. I drifted off easily, my body thankful for rest. But now, I'm gently stirred awake by the warm weight of a hand at my hip. A whisper breaks through the quiet.

"Zara…"

I turn to face him, eyes still adjusting. "You need something?" I murmur.

"Yes."

I sit up, instinctively ready to help—but he takes my hand and guides me toward the reason he's awake.

"I need you," he says, voice low, thick with desire.

A rush moves through me as I fully wake.

This man—this beautiful, strong, wounded man—is laid out before me, needing me. His body, usually a fortress of motion, is still. He's nearly helpless.

"That means you're all mine to do with as I please?" I ask, a teasing grin tugging at my lips.

The moonlight spilling in from the tall window catches his favorite dimple as he chuckles—a sound low and dangerous and sexy as hell.

He wants to play. So do I.

I lean down, brushing kisses over his cheek, letting my lips linger on the scratch of his stubble.

"Mmm," he groans. "Don't tease me too long."

"Oh, I will."

My hand finds him—hard, hot, impossibly ready. He shivers beneath my touch.

I climb on top, straddling him slowly, letting my thighs press against his still-powerful torso.

"Damn," he murmurs, voice strained. "You're so wet."

And then, in a blink, he grips my hips—tight, commanding—taking back control the only way he can.

He enters me with a gasp that escapes both of us.

He thrusts.

Deep.

Full.

I toss my head back, biting my lip, and ride him, slowly at first, savoring the heat, the stretch, the way we still fit—like we were built for this.

For each other.

His hands stay locked to my hips, guiding me, grounding me. Even wounded, he makes me feel like I'm the one who's being consumed.

This isn't just sex. It's a reclamation.

A return.

A promise.

And I don't want it to end

SIXTY-SIX

S atisfied, with my head resting on Jaxon's chest, I listen to the steady rhythm of his heart. The sun is just beginning to rise, and we've been talking about everything. I told him about Trey, about my father, about my sisters.

"Are you clear-eyed about it?" he asks, sounding exactly like a professional athlete. That's something I've come to respect about Jaxon—how he thinks. He always weighs his actions, considers the possible outcomes before making a move. I get it. That's what it means to play at the highest level. It's easy to armchair coach or play pretend. But the real work? That's something else entirely.

It's not so different from my career, I realize.

That's why my brows furrow as I seriously consider his question. I respect everything that comes out of his mouth—even the things that used to annoy me—because they're almost always laced with some kernel of wisdom.

"What do you mean?" I ask, wanting to understand what's behind the question.

"Do you understand why you helped your father?"

I rest my chin on top of my hands, which are stacked on his chest. We look into each other's eyes.

"I guess… because he's my father."

"Do you forgive him?" Jaxon asks, no hesitation.

I sigh, thoughtful. "That's a good question. When I first heard from my brother, Trey, that my dad was sick, I didn't want to hear it. I didn't want to care. I went to a drugstore that day and was planning to shoplift something. But for some reason, I didn't. And then I started thinking… about the kinds of things I've always taken. And it hit me—that my shoplifting was the little girl inside me, trying to steal what she was denied. Bookbags. Lipstick. Pens. Barrettes. Even face cream."

"Wow," Jaxon says softly. "That's… really insightful."

His praise warms me. That compliment—coming from him—feels huge. And true.

"Thank you, Jaxon."

Like I weigh nothing, he shifts me gently, guiding me back on top of his solid body—and the parts of him that are newly alert.

"You're welcome, babe," he says.

My eyes go wide in mock surprise. "Babe? Wow. I'm in the pocket now?"

He kisses me, slow and tender. "You're deep in the pocket."

"Wait," I say, stiffening as something important resurfaces—something I'd forgotten in the whirlwind of our reunion.

Jaxon's full attention is on me, and part of me basks in it. Maybe I should just let it go. But what if, once everything between us settles, there's a side of him that could break my heart—all because I didn't follow through on something I shouldn't have ignored?

His brow furrows. "What is it?"

My lips falter. I hate even bringing it up. "While you were gone… when I thought you'd ghosted me, I had your SUV returned to your apartment. It should be in your garage now." I pause. The space between his eyes tightens.

"Your coat was in the back seat," I continue, hesitating. "And I, um… went through your pockets." I shut my eyes for a second, bracing for judgment. "I found a note. From someone named Rach. She said she wanted you to…"

"Oh," he says, cutting in, his voice oddly relieved. "She gave that to Jake to pass along at the party we went to a few weeks ago. I meant to throw it away. Just forgot."

Relief floods me. "Oh."

He touches my face, brushing a thumb along one corner of my mouth, then the other. His eyebrows lift slightly, like he's savoring the feel of my skin.

"You never have to worry about another woman," he says. "I'm with you. And when I'm with someone, I'm loyal. Sure, I had hookups before—but I never committed. When I commit, Zara, I commit. And I'm committed to you."

"Same," I whisper, my heart spinning from the weight of his words.

We hold each other's gaze, and I feel like I could fall right through him. Like I've known him all my life. Like we've lived a thousand lifetimes together. And still, we're only just beginning.

Then he leans back against the pillows, the hint of a grin playing at his lips. "But let's not get distracted yet." He winks. "I want to hear the rest—all about your victory with your dad."

I smile, soaking it all in—this man, this moment. I believe him. I believe everything he just said. And I think about how close I came to never knowing any of it. What if I'd written him off completely? What if I hadn't let myself see past the surface? I hated him, once. Fiercely. But now... now I love him even more deeply than I ever despised him.

"To answer your question," I say, eyes steady on his, "Yes. I forgive my dad... because I forgave myself."

And with that, Jaxon shifts beneath me, guiding

me onto him with slow, assured hands. It's all heat and connection and rhythm, our bodies speaking a language all their own.

And just before I can catch my next breath—

"Mmm…" he's inside me again.

SUPERBOWL SUNDAY

Troy **"Big Talk" Blanchard:**
"It's cold. There's snow. But these stands? Blazing hot tonight."

Wes Ramsey:

"They're hot indeed, Troy. We're five minutes out from the third quarter… and Jaxon Wilde—whoa."

Troy:

"I'mma say it. I'm going out on a limb."

Wes:

"Oh no…"

Troy:

"Yeah, I'm saying it. In the history of this game, nobody—and I mean nobody—has ever played up to the level Wild Man is playing tonight. Two touchdowns. 124 yards carried in the first half. He's not just hot, he's volcanic. Ever since that injury, it's like he came back possessed."

Wes:

"That's true, Troy. They call him Wild Man for a reason. Two touchdowns, wow! And I think his lady might have something to do with it."

The Jumbotron flashes a shot of Zara Morgan, bundled up in an oversized Bull Sharks windbreaker, front row, beaming.

Wes:

"There she is—Zara Morgan. Thumbs up. That's their thing. Their signal."

Split screen: Jaxon, on the sideline, spots her. His grin spreads, dimple deep. He flashes the thumbs up right back.

Troy:

"She's been at every single game since he returned —home *and* away. Word is she's basically part of the organization now. The players love her. The wives. Coaching staff. Everybody."

Wes:

"And we do too. She's been electric. Only person in this stadium screaming louder than her…"

Troy:

"…is her father."

Wes:

"Great story there. Zara and her dad reconnected after he was hospitalized last year. Now? They're tight. He's been at practices. Games."

Troy:

"Guy was on his deathbed—and look at him now."

The Jumbotron cuts to Leo, face peeking from the hood of his heavy Bull Sharks parka. He flashes a proud thumbs up. Beside him: Zara, Trey, Linda, and Bloom all wrap their arms around him, smiling through the cold.

Wes:

"What a moment."

Cut to Jaxon, clapping, focused. His voice carries all the way to the front rows:

Jaxon (shouting):

"Let's go! Let's finish the job!"

SIXTY-EIGHT

TWO-MINUTE WARNING

"Oh my God," I keep repeating, fingers crossed inside the sleeves of my coat.

This game has been a nail-biter, and I've seen them all—haven't missed one since Jaxon returned to the field. I made the decision early on not to sit in the luxury box, even though the team offered. It was too far removed from him. I wanted to be close, close enough to feel like I was in it with him without disturbing his focus.

The past seventeen weeks have been a whirlwind. A good one. And honestly, I don't care what social media says—about me not having a life of my own, about me orbiting around a man. Let them talk. This is what Jaxon and I do: we show up for each other.

Watching him out there now, helmet low, shoulders squared, Bull Sharks three down and thirty-three yards from the end zone, I finally understand what Genesis meant when she said our men need us *in* the game with them. We're supposed to breathe them, live them, ride with them. I won't take it quite that far —not without equal energy in return—but Jaxon is my gladiator.

The first down begins.

There's a charged silence in the air, like every person in the stadium is holding their breath.

I can't make out what Micah's calling, but I can tell he's changed the play. The ball is snapped.

My eyes find Jaxon immediately. His defender, Antonio Gill, is clinging to him like static, but the play shifts direction and ends with Myles Jones picking up four yards.

Second and six.

The players reset at the line of scrimmage.

"This is it!" my dad yells beside me, his voice strong and clear. You'd never guess he was once so sick he couldn't lift his head. A bacterial infection nearly took him out, but now he's shouting with the energy of a teenager.

We've had long talks since that day I first visited him in the hospital. That afternoon was nearly as nerve-wracking as this game. Jaxon couldn't come— he had rehab—but it was better that way. It needed to be just us.

When I walked into that room, my father looked at me like he was seeing a ghost.

"You look so much like her," he said, before breaking down into tears.

He meant my mother. And to witness a man I'd known my whole life as emotionally unavailable fall apart like that—it changed something in me. I crossed the room and hugged him without hesitation. I surprised even myself.

He asked me to listen—just listen—while he explained everything. No sugarcoating. No trying to make it easier for me to digest.

He told me he and my mother believed raising kids was women's work. That was their agreement. And when she died, he panicked and rushed to fill the void. That's how Stacy came into the picture.

He said he ignored the signs because he believed women were inherently kind. He'd let that belief cloud his judgment.

"Then we had three more, and Stacy just wasn't pulling her weight. I ended up doing everything for them. She liked being out of the house, and… she had a few affairs. By the time I realized you needed me to step in and really pay attention, it was too late. You'd already left." He shook his head. "I'm sorry I let her treat you the way she did. She was…" He trailed off.

I rubbed his shoulder, offering him a small comfort. "No need to speak ill of the dead, Dad. But that was an astute take," I said. "Did Trey help you come to that conclusion?"

He laughed, then nodded. "Yeah. He did."

"He's been shrinking the hell out of me too," I said.

We both laughed. That was the moment I told him I understood. That I forgave him. That I wanted to leave behind his guilt—and my own anger—and see what might be possible for us going forward.

We shook on it. Hugged on it.

And a week later, he was out of the hospital.

He moved in with me to make it easier to get to his appointments. And when Jaxon was in town, they went to rehab together at the team's facility. The staff even treated my dad when Jaxon was away. I don't think they made a big deal about it. They just did it. Because that's what families do when they form— when they rebuild.

Now here he is, at full volume, shouting like a coach from the stands, stronger than he's been in years. He's living and breathing this game like he's in it, like we all are.

Micah's voice calls out the hike.

The ball's in his hands.

Everything moves quickly—players shifting, defenders scrambling. I zero in on Jaxon, just as the pass arcs through the air. It's perfect.

He catches it.

And then he runs.

I'm up on my feet, bouncing, hands on my head, eyes wide.

"Go, go, go," I whisper-shout, almost afraid to be too loud. I want this for him so badly. I want him to finish it.

Antonio Gill is closing in, fast. I'm silently begging him not to take Jaxon down hard—not to twist something, not to cause more injury.

Then, it happens.

Jaxon dives, pushing past the last line of defense. He hits the grass, rolls, bounces up like a bolt of lightning, ball in hand, knees pumping as the rest of the team collapses onto him in celebration.

The screen flashes: **TOUCHDOWN.**

The stadium explodes with sound.

My dad is howling. Trey, Linda, and Bloom are screaming, and I can barely keep from falling to my knees. My hands cover my mouth. My whole body is shaking.

The team rushes to line up and spike the ball.

The clock is running out.

Game over.

We won.

And then I see him.

Jaxon is breaking free of the celebration, running —limping just a little—right to me. He's dodging the press, his teammates, anyone who tries to stop him.

I lean over the edge of the stands.

He reaches up, pulls me into his arms.

We're kissing. Holding on for dear life.

"We won!" I shout, laughing, near tears.

"We won," he says again, breathless against my mouth.

And we did. We really, truly did.

EPILOGUE

THREE MONTHS LATER

I hate these scenes—the ones I have to play with Blaine. Sorry... Toby Lane. To this day, I still don't understand what's wrong with Blaine Bello. What are we, in the 1950s? When actors had to contort themselves to fit narrow-minded ideas of what made someone "acceptable"? I never realized how much not being his real self had affected Blaine. It might explain why he burns down every relationship he touches.

"This is my family's company..." I lean in, frowning hard. "My father's legacy. You're just some guy who showed up out of obscurity, and now you think you can call the shots? Bullshit."

By the end of the line, Blaine and I are practically nose to nose.

He slowly leans back, snorts viciously, and snarls, "Whatever this tantrum is, it's going to get you nowhere."

I grunt. "It's not a tantrum, Peter. It's not even a warning. I'm telling you: get in your spot" —I point to the floor— "and know your fucking place."

His eyes go glassy and crossed, staring daggers at me. That's exactly how it's written in the script.

"And cut! Let's take five."

"He's here again?" Blaine says, instantly, glaring over my shoulder.

I turn to see Jaxon standing near the director's monitor. He flashes me a thumbs-up and a wink. I return the gesture.

"This isn't a football game," Blaine mutters.

"Oh, grow up," I sigh.

Rumor is, Blaine's days are numbered on this show. Between the bad behavior and the trail of broken hearts he leaves in production, no one's surprised. Lately, he's taken aim at his next target, another intern barely out of college. But when Jaxon shows up, he gets extra pissy.

"I don't even understand why Chris is letting him on set," Blaine grumbles. "It's a distraction. We're trying to shoot."

I give him a cheerful, exaggerated smile. "Because everyone loves Jaxon. Just get with the program, Blaine. Let go of your envy and fall in love with him too."

"Envy? And it's Toby," he mutters the last part like it's still a secret. Please.

Before I can respond, Pat, the stage director, arrives.

"Toby, I'm going to need you to step over there," she says, hand on his shoulder.

"For what?"

"Chris changed the scene. That's where he wants you now."

"Nobody told me about any changes," Blaine snaps. "What am I supposed to do with that, huh?"

I groan and tip my head back. He has a point, but his delivery is exhausting.

"Just go, Toby," I say. "He's the director. Roll with it."

Blaine eventually sulks off. That's when Joe London, Paige Nelson, and Tillman Ford storm the stage like they're mid-scene. But there's something off.

"Then *you* do it," Joe growls, throwing up his hands.

"I don't *want* to do it," Paige snaps, clutching her chest.

Tillman massages his temples. "You're both cowards."

Blaine and I exchange a confused look. We're not done with our scene. What is this?

Then, out of nowhere, all three of them drop to one knee in front of me. Their hands extend, palms stacked like a ceremonial offering. Paige's hand is on top, and resting on it is a small, plush, royal-blue ring box.

My jaw drops.

Blaine huffs beside me like he's already figured it out. And he has.

Jaxon strides out onto the stage, confident, radiant, completely mine.

He takes the box from my costars, all of whom are grinning ear to ear.

"I'll do it," he says.

Tears well in my eyes and spill freely. I never imagined this moment. Never thought I'd want to share a bathroom, let alone a life, with someone. But this man —I would go anywhere with him. Forever.

He opens the box. His eyes glisten. "Beautiful, would you marry me?"

"Absolutely," I whisper, not even needing a beat.

"I'm out of here!" Blaine groans, stomping away.

We don't even look at him. The applause is thunderous. I'm kissing Jaxon again, tasting joy, commitment, and the future all at once.

www.ingramcontent.com/pod-product-compliance
Lightning Source LLC
Chambersburg PA
CBHW051957240626
47153CB00005B/1787